Amish Days

Hope's Story

A Three-Story-Bundle Amish Romance

Brenda Maxfield

Hollybrook Amish Romance

Tica House Publishing
Anderson, Indiana

Tica House Publishing
www.brendamaxfield.com

Publisher's Note: This is a work of fiction. Names, characters, places, and incidents are a product of the author's imagination. Locales and public names are sometimes used for atmospheric purposes. Any resemblance to actual people, living or dead, or to businesses, companies, events, institutions, or locales is completely coincidental.

Amish Days Hope's Story/ Brenda Maxfield. -- 1st ed.
ISBN-13: 978-1514120750

Table of Contents

.

Missing Abram

One

The counsel of the LORD standeth forever,
the thoughts of his heart to all generations.
Psalm 33:11 (King James Version)

The hard-working horse whinnied and stomped her hoof in the dust.

"Hush, Chocolate," Hope murmured, absently rubbing the white spot above the mare's nose. She squinted in the bright sunlight, her thick lashes doing little to shade her honey-brown eyes. "Just a few minutes more. I promise."

Three bags of chicken feed were tucked into the buggy — chicken feed that wasn't necessary. Hope's father had several bags of feed stored in the back corner of the barn where three cats dutifully chased the mice away.

But what other excuse did Hope have for going to the Feed & Supply on a hot Tuesday morning? And she *did* need an excuse.

For Tuesday was the day Abram Lambright went for supplies.

Chocolate nuzzled Hope's shoulder, but she didn't notice. An approaching buggy had her full attention. She recognized the

Lambright's road horse, Sprint. The old mare could no longer trot a straight line. She veered left, forcing whoever drove her to exercise a strong hand and a quick wit.

Hope's heart sang. *Abram.*

A light breeze caught the soft brown curls at her ears, blowing them across her cheeks. She hurriedly tucked them back under her *kapp.* She licked her bottom lip and forced herself to be calm. She'd known Abram for years. No reason to get riled up at the sight of his tall silhouette and broad shoulders now.

No reason at all.

Besides, she shouldn't notice such things.

Sprint's unsteady clip—clop came closer and Hope's excitement plummeted. It wasn't Abram driving the buggy at all, but rather his younger brother Daniel with his little sister, Mercy.

"Hi, Hope!" Mercy half-stood in the jolting buggy and waved wildly until a rut in the road plopped her back onto the seat.

Hope swallowed her disappointment. "Hi, back," she called to her young friend.

Daniel pulled on the reins and guided Sprint to a stop. Mercy hurtled out of the buggy and skipped over. "Where's Abram?" she asked, turning her freckled face and green eyes toward Hope.

"What do you mean where's Abram? I was going to ask you the same thing."

"He's not home. *Mamm* said you might know since he's sweet on you."

Hope's cheeks burned. *Had Abram's mother been watching?*

Daniel joined them. He seemed jumpy and though he smiled at her, it didn't hide the look of concern in his eyes. Hope's stomach tensed.

"What's this about Abram? Where is he?" she asked.

Daniel shuffled his feet in the dirt and wouldn't meet her eyes. Hope touched his forearm. "Where is he?" she asked again.

"Likely off doing chores. It's nothing," Daniel answered. "Come on, Mercy, we've got to get moving or *Mamm* will never trust us to come again."

Mercy's eyes widened. "Sorry, Hope. I have to go."

"Wait. Aren't your *mamm* and *dat* worried? Is Abram in some kind of trouble?"

Daniel took Mercy by the shoulders and shuffled her up the steps of the shop. "See you, Hope," he called over his shoulder.

Mercy wiggled loose and ran back to Hope, her light blue dress billowing around skinny legs. "They think he's back with the *Englischers*."

Hope frowned and nausea stormed through her. "What? But why? I don't understand. He came back from his *rumspringa* months ago."

"Mercy!" Daniel's voice was sharp.

Mercy turned. "I'm coming!"

Hope watched Daniel open the shop door for Mercy and heard the clank from the old rusted bell hanging just inside. They disappeared behind the windowed door.

Beads of sweat lined Hope's upper lip. Hardly mid-morning and the Indiana sun was already beating down with a vengeance. She swiped the moisture away and climbed into the buggy. Lost in thought, she batted at the circling flies, took up the reins, and clucked her tongue at Chocolate to start home. Her thin body erect, she paid no mind as her *kapp* slipped back a bit over the chestnut braid she'd twisted and pinned up earlier that morning.

Endless fields of tall stalks of corn bordered the road like massive walls of green, creating the feel of a narrow covered bridge. All was quiet except the soft rustle of wind and steady rhythm of Chocolate's hooves beating the pavement.

Uneasiness poured over Hope like molasses. Where was Abram? What was he doing? Was he all right? Why wasn't Daniel talking?

But most important of all, why hadn't Abram told *her* he was leaving?

****

Back home, Hope took care of the buggy, stroked Chocolate, and then turned her out into the field. She rushed, worry over Abram riddling her nerves.

Inside the house, her aunt Ruth sat in the rocker on the multi-colored rug Hope and her mother had braided two years before. Ruth fanned herself with a dishtowel and smiled when Hope burst through the door. "Going to be miserable hot today," she observed, her crooked front tooth making her look much younger than her forty-three years.

Hope nodded. She liked Ruth—liked the happy spirit she brought to the house. But right then she was distracted by the pain beginning in her ankle. She hurried to the wooden staircase where she took the steps two at a time up to the bedroom she shared with her seventeen-year-old sister, Mary.

"Hope!" Ruth called after her. "Are you limping again? What's wrong?"

Yes, she was limping again, but she hated to admit it. Ever since a disastrous fall off a plow horse at age three, Hope's ankle registered stress with pain and a limp. Just like Grandmother's arthritic knees warned everyone of an impending storm.

Hope pushed the bedroom door closed behind her and crossed the smooth plank floor to pull out the middle drawer of her dresser. She reached under her stockings and retrieved a folded piece of paper.

She sank onto the bed and carefully opened the note, pressing it flat on her lap.

Hope, I missed seeing you last year when I was gone on

rumspringa for so long.

> *I enjoy hearing your voice at Sunday Night Singing.*
>
> *Abram*

Abram had slipped her the note during the singing just two days before, and she'd hardly stopped reading it since. She harbored the idea that it was a sort of love note.

But if it was a love note, and if he was interested in her, wouldn't he have told her he was leaving? Especially if he was returning to the *Englischers*, like Mercy implied? Hope knew all about the family he'd spent time with during his *rumspringa*. She knew all about the new best friend he'd made. Robby. Robby Wallace, whose father owned some sort of factory and was rolling in money. Or so Abram had reported.

Hope had seen the fire of yearning in Abram's eyes when he spoke of them, and her stomach had soured with dread. Abram hadn't been baptized into the church since returning. What was he waiting for? Did he want to become an outsider? An *Englischer*? And if he wanted to leave the community, how were the two of them ever to court or marry?

Hope chided herself. Not that he'd asked her. Not that he'd done anything really, except make sure he spoke to her after Sunday singing and every Tuesday when she found some excuse to be outside the Feed & Supply.

Yet now, there *was* the note.

Every other Sunday after every youth singing, Hope prayed that he would ask to give her a ride home in his buggy. But he never did. Not once.

She slumped back on the shadow quilt covering her bed and pressed Abram's note to her heart. The white curtains flanking the window stirred as a hot, heavy breeze moved through the room. Who was she kidding? Abram wasn't interested in her. He probably thought of her as another sister.

Quick tears pricked her eyes and a sense of loss moved up her throat. Abram was so strong, so kind, so everything she wanted. And it was time. She was old enough to be courted. Old enough to be in love and promised.

Old enough to be married.

Matthew 6:33 flashed through her mind. *But seek ye first the kingdom of God, and his righteousness; and all these things shall be added unto you.*

Would marriage be added unto her? And children? And her own home?

She closed her eyes and took a slow, even breath to quiet her racing heart. She had to be honest with herself. What she really wanted was Abram added unto her.

It was Abram she wanted.

Two

Abram sat on the edge of a padded lounge chair next to a tiled kidney-shaped pool.

"Relax, man," Robby said. He clapped his friend on the back. "Do all Amish take everything so seriously? You make me tired."

Abram took a moment before speaking. "I can't answer for all Amish. Do all *Englischers* take nothing seriously?"

"Touché," Robby said and laughed.

Abram tugged at the neck of his factory uniform. *Englisch* clothes still felt strange to him. After wearing them so often during his *rumspringa*, he figured he'd be used to them. But still, they itched and just felt wrong.

"How long are you here for this time?" Robby asked. He grabbed a can of soda from the ice bucket sitting on the patio table and offered it to Abram.

Abram accepted the drink and popped it open. He took a long, deep swig, relishing the cold liquid on such a sweltering day. "A few weeks at least. Maybe a bit more. Then I have to return—*Dat* will need me in the fields." Abram ran a hand through wavy hair so dark, it was almost black. "He probably needs me now…"

"I'm surprised you came again. Don't get me wrong—I'm glad you're here. But I thought you already had enough money for another horse and whatever else you were saving for. Do other Amish guys use their *rumspringa* or however you call it to earn money? I thought it was to run around and be wild." Robby stretched out his long legs and propped his bare feet on the table. "Is that why you're back? Because you missed being free?"

Abram stiffened. "I am free."

There was an edge to his voice, and Robby raised his hands in mock surrender. "Sorry, man. Didn't mean anything by it."

"I know." Abram rubbed his strong, calloused palms over the thick plastic arms of the chair. "You let me stay in your guest house, and your father is letting me work the factory line. I'm grateful."

"But…"

Abram's smoky-gray eyes gazed into the clear sky. "But."

"It's the girl, isn't it?"

Abram pressed his lips together and didn't answer. He should have told Hope. He should have declared his intentions. He wondered what she was thinking. Did she even know he was gone? Did she care?

He stared at Robby's cell phone lying on the glass table and wished he could call her. Hear her sweet voice. Tell her he had a plan. That his purpose was solid.

But the closest phone to Hope was in a shanty five miles from her house in front of the Feed & Supply. He gave a rueful smile. Wouldn't someone be surprised if the phone there started ringing, and he asked to speak to Hope Lehman?

"What's so funny?" Robby asked.

"Thinking of home," Abram said. He stood and set the empty soda can on the table. "I'm going to change clothes."

He strode around the pool toward a small cottage situated at the back of the expansive yard. Before he got there, Robby's redheaded sister Rene emerged from the pool house to his right, wearing a gauze cover-up over a fire-red bikini.

"Abram, there you are!" Her voice tinkled like wind chimes. "Want to take a dip with me?"

Abram averted his eyes. "No, thanks," he said and proceeded to the door of the cottage.

Rene gave a light giggle. "Why am I not surprised?" she called after him.

Abram shut the cottage door and leaned against the cool wood.

His quarters were cold and the hum of central air sounded like the low whine of a tree full of cicadas. He sank to the edge of the sprawling bed.

What was he doing here? His people didn't mix with outsiders. Not like this. He pulled again at the neck of his uniform.

But his plan wouldn't work without money, and he couldn't put the burden for help on his father. Maybe another time, but not after last year's crop. And the factory work paid well. Very well. Better than anything near Hollybrook. Up north, many Amish worked in factories, but not in his community. The Amish near Hollybrook had remained farmers, and according to his father, that was the way it would stay.

He folded his uniform in a neat pile on the bedside table. With relief, he stepped back into his own clothes. There would be no church at home that Sunday, but the following weekend, he'd arrange for a van to take him back so he could attend service.

So he could see Hope again.

Three

Hope sat at the long wooden table staring into a large plastic bowl of green beans. If she grabbed three at once, she could take the ends off them with two snaps instead of six—getting herself out of the sweltering house faster. Maybe she'd have time to escape to the stand of oak trees out back for a while.

Mary stood at the sink, humming.

"What are you so happy about?" Hope asked.

Mary turned, her hands dripping on the rag rug. "The Lambrights have a nephew. He might be coming to stay with them."

"How does that concern you?" Hope asked.

Mary grabbed up a dishtowel, rushed over, and plopped down on the bench opposite her. "You can say that because you have Abram. I have no one!"

Hope sucked in her breath. She'd been doing so well—keeping Abram out of her waking thoughts. At night, though, his strong-boned face haunted her. His warm smile. His charcoal eyes staring into hers. And two nights before, she'd thought she heard his deep laugh. But it was only Mary, groaning and tossing in the bed next to hers.

"Are you listening to me?" Mary asked.

Hope stood quickly, nearly toppling the bench behind her. "I'm always listening," she said. Compassion for her sister filled her heart. She understood only too well Mary's desires. "Beans are done. I'm going outside."

"*Mamm* and Ruth will be back soon. They expect us to have the table set and dinner cooking. Plus we haven't made the sugar cream pie yet. You know I can't make a crust as flaky as yours."

"I'll be back in time." Hope gave her sister's shoulder a gentle squeeze. Then she pulled off her apron and tossed it onto the back of the rocker. The screen door squawked as she stepped outside. She inhaled the muggy air, feeling a tightness low in her lungs.

Dear Gott, please help me to keep my eyes on You. Help me not to get distracted with things that don't concern me.

Nearly two weeks had passed, and she'd not heard one grain of news. If Abram didn't show up for the church meeting that Sunday, everyone would know he'd left. People already wondered why he'd been gone on *rumspringa* for so long the year before. And why hadn't he accepted baptism the minute he'd returned? The Lambrights were strangely silent on the whole business.

Which was odd in itself.

Hope yearned to talk to Mercy. If the Lambrights had learned anything, Mercy would tell her. Hope wandered behind the house and headed toward the oaks. She walked slowly, favoring her right ankle. It had been bothering her since she'd found out Abram had disappeared.

The ankle—her public announcement that something was wrong. Again, she wondered why all her stress had to reveal itself in such an obvious way. When she attempted to hide the pain or the limp, it was worse. Well, she'd have to disguise it somehow on Sunday when Abram didn't show. It was embarrassing enough that her family knew how troubled she was. She didn't need to alert the entire community.

Under the shade of the oaks, the temperature was cooler by a few degrees. Hope sank onto the mound of grass she had retreated to since childhood. She leaned against the rough bark of the largest oak tree and looked at the tiny lumps of soil scattered about, now overgrown with grass. They made up her miniature cemetery. When she was barely six, she had discovered a dead bluebird next to the barn. Its little body was limp and its beak was pressed open in a perpetual cry for help.

Without telling mother, she'd carried it gently in the folds of her apron out to the stand of oaks where she'd buried it with a prayer and a song. Since that day, she'd buried an assortment of dead animals—mostly found out in the fields, but sometimes in the barn.

Hope's muscles began to relax. *Gott, please help Abram, wherever he is. Help him see the error of his—*

She paused. That was a daring prayer. And prideful. It wasn't her place to judge. She didn't even know what Abram was doing. She began again, *Dear Gott, please bless Abram. Help him to rest in your love and safety—*

"There you are," Mary interrupted, entering the shaded area.

Hope jerked with surprise.

"Don't be angry at my intrusion." Mary sat next to Hope and curled her short legs under herself. Her gaze was penetrating. "What's wrong?"

Hope put on a smile. "Nothing. It's too hot in the house. Even the porch is wilty."

Mary rested her fingers on Hope's arm, and at her tender touch, Hope's throat filled with tears. She shook her head and blinked away the moisture in her eyes.

"It's Abram, isn't it?" Mary whispered.

Hope nodded. She couldn't blink fast enough to stop the tears now, and they puddled on her cheeks. "He's gone," she said.

Mary sighed. "Stories are circulating."

Hope clutched Mary's sleeve. "What are people saying?"

"That he didn't get enough of *rumspringa*. That he's got an *Englisch* girl..."

Hope covered her mouth.

Mary waved her hand in dismissal. "Just idle talk." She looked deeply into her sister's shadowed eyes. "It *is* idle talk, right?"

Hope looked down at her lap. "I don't know."

"He'll be here for Sunday meeting?"

"I don't know." Hope was silent for a moment, and then she sat up a bit straighter. "It's not my concern, though, is it? We're not courting. He's a friend. Nothing more."

She stood and shook out the folds of her blue dress. Bits of leaves sprinkled to the earth. "Enough moping. Let's go cook."

Mary scrambled up beside her. "*Jah*, let's."

****

That next Sunday, Hope sat sandwiched between Mary and their younger sister, Ann, on the way to the Burkholder's house for church. Ann jabbered on and on about the new tricks she was teaching Apple, their new white-and-brown-speckled puppy. Hope tried to pay attention, but her stomach felt as if it held a block of ice.

Mamm had stayed home, complaining of a headache. She rarely missed church, and things felt odd without her. Aunt Ruth sat with *Dat* in the front of the buggy—her continual jabbering matching Ann's.

Dat pulled into the yard and parked their buggy alongside the Troyers. They weren't late, but already there was a solid row of buggies in place. Ann jumped out and Hope followed. Her eyes scanned the pockets of people making their way inside.

Adrenaline flashed through her body. *There he was*, easily taller than most of the men milling near the door. She couldn't help but notice how handsome he looked, how at ease and naturally he carried himself. He turned and their eyes met. He smiled with what looked like real pleasure, but Hope became so flustered, she couldn't return the gesture. All she felt was a muddle of confusion. His smile faded as he studied her.

A jumble of emotions churned through her heart. How could he leave without a word and then give her such a heartfelt smile as if nothing was amiss? Didn't he know how she had worried? How she had wondered? A surge of anger unbalanced Hope, and she clasped her hands to her chest. She hadn't expected anger.

His gaze unnerved her. She shuddered, but she knew she couldn't keep standing there like a hitching post all morning. Finally, she walked toward the house, deciding her best course of action would be to play calm and ignore him.

Mary pulled on her sleeve and scuttled to keep up.

Just as Hope reached the porch, Abram stepped close and cleared his throat. She paused.

"Hope, you're here." There was a warm familiarity in his husky voice.

Her anger resurfaced, and she turned to him. "Of course I'm here. I'm not the one who left!"

She clamped her lips shut. What was she thinking? Did she have to blurt out her thoughts, especially with such biting words? Did she have no control?

Mary gave a low murmur and hustled Ann ahead of her into the house.

The pleasure Abram had shown at seeing her only moments before evaporated. "I won't be away as long this time," he said, and his voice faltered.

"So you're not staying even now?" Hope asked, her tone still harsh.

"You're angry?"

"Why should I be? It doesn't make any difference to me." She forced nonchalance, and the effort left her breathless.

"You're angry." He repeated, and this time, it wasn't a question.

She stiffened, now wanting nothing more than to escape. Shame pulsed through her. She worked to school her expression— to hide her hurt and anger.

He didn't move.

She took a long breath. "Besides, why should I be angry? We're just friends."

If that were true, why did she feel so awful?

Abram took a step back and regarded her. She saw the confusion in his eyes, and a cloud of regret settled into her stomach. She blinked rapidly, searching for a way to take back the last five minutes. She opened her mouth, but nothing came out.

"I have my reasons," he said. He bent slightly toward her, and Hope's heart quickened at his closeness.

"Does anyone know your reasons?" Her voice was quieter now.

"Not entirely."

"Mercy was worried about you."

Abram's brow drew into a frown. "I didn't intend that."

I was worried about you, too, she wanted to say. But, she didn't. She'd been living in a dream world of fantasy and romance, a world no more real to her than the *Englischer's* world.

Abram shifted his weight from one foot to the other as if deciding whether to tell her something. She struggled to hide the yearning that quickly crowded the anger from her heart. If he saw it, it would embarrass them both.

He paused, then sighed. He turned away to stride into the house.

Hope stared after him. She took a jagged breath and slowly followed, moving to the unmarried women's section of the meeting room. She perched on one of the wooden benches like a stone and stretched out her throbbing ankle, ignoring the pain.

A heavy tightness squeezed her chest. What had she done? Had her hard words killed any hope of something more with Abram?

Now she would likely live long and lonely and steeped in regret. A muscle quivered in her jaw. Would she eventually have to watch him court someone else? Marry someone else? Would she have to pretend to be happy for them?

Every fiber in her body was acutely aware of him across the room. She tried to swallow past the ball of wool in her throat, tried to ignore the tears threatening to spill. She squirmed, forcing his image from her eyes, her mind, and her heart. She had to get out of there. She had to get out of there fast.

But how? She could hardly run out of worship.

Mary elbowed her, inched close, and whispered, "What is wrong with you? And why were you so mean to Abram?"

Hope tried again to swallow. She was acting the fool.

Enough.

So Abram probably disliked her now. Maybe more than disliked her. He likely thought she was mean and awful. But how would that change her life? He didn't figure into her days.

Not even a little.

She sucked air.

But he did. *He did.* Thoughts of him were with her every minute of every day. A tear slid down her cheek, and she swiped at it. She grasped a worn copy of the *Ausbund* close to her chest like a lifeline. The frayed cover and tattered pages filled with songs pressed against her hands. Singing was her favorite part of church. She willed herself to think on that.

To think on anything but Abram.

Gott, I'm here to worship you. May I please you with my prayers and with my voice. May I think on you, not on others. Gott, please help me.

She closed her eyes. God would help her. She took a slow, even breath. Everything would be all right. God was in control.

Four

Abram climbed into Robby's low sports car after a long day at the factory. He sank into the seat and buckled himself in.

"How was your weekend?" Robby asked, shifting the car into gear.

"Fine."

"Did you see that girl?"

Abram nodded.

"How'd it go?"

"It didn't." Abram closed his lips and attempted to put the thought of Hope from his mind. His meeting with her had ungrounded him. He'd foolishly thought she would be happy to see him.

How wrong he'd been.

His plan was tumbling. He might as well return home to Hollybrook and stay, but he'd promised Robby's father another two weeks of work.

And he wouldn't go back on his word.

When Abram had told his own father he'd be gone two more weeks, his *dat* had reacted with anger. But his *mamm* had been relieved. Happy even.

Which had nothing to do with the two more weeks.

His *mamm* had been overcome with relief upon learning that his leaving had nothing to do with *rumspringa*. He could have told her he'd be gone two more years, and she would have smiled.

The day before, after the church meeting was finished, Abram had tried to talk again with Hope. When the meal was served, he'd looked all over and finally spotted her sitting in the middle of her family. She was so tightly surrounded that he didn't consider breaking through.

Besides, she'd made it clear; she wanted nothing to do with him.

He could almost hear the cracking foundation of his dream, almost hear the beams slamming to the ground.

And here he was, stuck in the *Englischer's* world for two more weeks.

Robby pulled into the long drive approaching his home. Abram marveled again at its grandeur. He'd been lucky to land there during his *rumspringa*. He knew that. Plus he knew that Robby's father's connection with his community's crops had paved the way. And Abram was grateful. Truly, he was. He had been able to accumulate a good amount of money from his work there. All part of his plan.

His broken, crushed plan.

"We're here," Robby announced, yanking up the parking brake.

"Think I'll hang out in the cottage if you don't mind," Abram said.

"Hey, suit yourself."

Abram climbed out of the car and headed through the house and out back to his cottage. He went inside, grateful the day was nearly over. Thirteen days left and counting.

A soft knock sounded, and he turned to face his half-open door.

Rene entered with an inviting smile on her face. "Hey, Amish boy. Want to go swimming?"

Abram rubbed the back of his neck. "No, thanks."

Rene stepped forward, her long, thin legs barefoot. "You're not going to make me swim alone, are you?" She tossed her thick hair over her shoulder, and her blue eyes gleamed.

"I don't swim."

"I know, but you can get in and splash around with me." She

reached out and touched his arm. He flinched, but she continued resting her fingers on his skin. "Ah, don't tell me you're still shy. We know each other well now."

Abram pulled his arm back. "We don't know each other at all."

"Come on, Abram. At least come outside with me and visit." She pursed her pink lips into an adorable pout.

"No, thanks," he repeated, walking to the door. He waited until she gave a grunt and pranced off.

Abram made sure the door was completely shut before he sat on the edge of his bed. There was no denying that Rene was cute. And fun-loving.

And available.

He clenched his teeth until they hurt. Why had Hope been so unfeeling? He thought she liked him. Didn't she always show up at Feed & Supply at the perfect time every Tuesday? That couldn't be a coincidence. Or could it?

He wasn't sure of anything anymore.

Something inside him stiffened. No, that wasn't true. He was sure of something. He was sure that he wasn't a quitter. Maybe his plan had taken a slight detour.

But it was *still* his plan, and he intended to work it.

Five

"He's here!" Mary grabbed Hope's arms and squeezed. "He's here!" She flew to their bedroom window and leaned out.

Hope followed and grabbed her sister's sleeve. "Are you crazy? If he sees you gawking like that, he'll run for the hills. And what happened here? Did you take the screen out of the window?"

"I had to. Otherwise, I couldn't get a good look. Don't worry, I'll put it back." Mary leaned a bit further, and Hope held her tight for fear she'd tumble right out.

"He's good-looking! Hope, see for yourself."

Hope gazed around Mary's shoulders to the scene below and had to agree. The Lambright's nephew was definitely handsome. He was tall, too, maybe taller than Abram.

Hope gulped. *Why bring Abram into it?*

Mary smoothed her dress and tucked a stray curl under her *kapp*. Hope watched her primp, fearing she was wandering close to pride. But then, hadn't pride been the reason for her ugly behavior with Abram the other day? She'd been hurt, and she'd opened her big mouth and pretended she didn't care. She was quite sure that counted as pride.

"Let's go down," she suggested, burying her shame to pray about it later.

Mary rushed ahead.

Mamm and Dat were welcoming Josiah, and Ruth was already serving tall glasses of lemonade. Ann was herding the puppy, Apple, out the door.

Daniel, Mercy, and Martha Lambright came in, scooting around Apple as she yipped and jumped.

"*Ach*, cute puppy!" cried Mercy.

"Want to help me with her?" asked Ann. The two girls disappeared outside.

"We're about ready to dish up!" *Mamm* called after them. Her cheeks blazed a ruddy red from bending over the stove in the smothering heat. But then, *Mamm's* cheeks were often flushed from hard work. And it was always more pronounced when people came over—being a hostess wasn't her favorite activity.

If it weren't for Ruth's presence, Hope knew they'd rarely, if ever, have guests.

"Where's Isaac?" *Dat* asked.

"He sends his regrets," Martha answered. "With Abram gone, he needs every minute."

"I told you I would stay and help," Josiah protested.

Martha waved her hand and chuckled. "Nonsense. You need to meet the community."

At Martha's comment, Mary poked Hope. Hope ignored her and pulled out a bench. "Shall we sit?" she asked.

After calling in the girls, Aunt Ruth organized everyone at the table laden with food. Ann and Mercy jabbered happily, squished together on the porch bench that had been pulled in for the occasion. Hope busied herself passing the heavy bowls of food. When she handed the mashed potatoes to her *dat*, she looked up to see Josiah staring at her.

She lowered her gaze to the table, hoping Mary hadn't noticed. But Mary must have noticed, for Hope heard her suck in her breath.

Mary quickly regained her composure, and a moment later, asked sweetly, "Josiah, how long will you be staying with the Lambrights?"

Josiah looked away from Hope to focus on Mary. "That's uncertain right now. It could be quite a while."

Martha Lambright patted his hand with her chubby fingers. "We hope it's a good long while."

Daniel nodded and grinned. "We can use the help."

Josiah looked again at Hope. "Mercy was bragging on you. She said you make the best pies."

Hope felt the blood rush to her cheeks, and she sensed Mary stiffen beside her. She didn't relish being the center of attention under any circumstances, but now seemed particularly awkward.

"Not really," she stammered. "Uh, Mary makes delicious pies."

Mercy's fork clattered on her plate. "*Jah*, you do, Hope. You know your pies are the best."

Mary's posture wilted. "*Jah*, Hope. We all know how *wunderbaar* your pies are."

Hope prayed no one else could hear the edge of hurt and sarcasm in Mary's voice.

Dat coughed and picked up the platter of pork chops. "Daniel, you better feed those bones of yours. Harvest is coming. You'll need all your strength."

Daniel grinned and grabbed the platter. "*Jah*, thank you."

For the rest of the meal, Hope kept her attention on her food, only looking up if spoken to. Gratefully, that didn't happen but once more when Ann asked her to save some table scraps for Apple.

Six

Hope stood outside the house, waiting for the rest of the family to emerge. The community wagon was coming by to take them to worship at the Miller's that Sunday, which saved *Dat* from harnessing Chocolate. The heat had lessened in the last couple days, and that morning a refreshing breeze rustled the tassels of corn. *Dat* warned that a storm was coming, but all looked peaceful.

The screen door squawked and Mary trudged down the steps to stand on the grass. She positioned herself a good distance away and set her face into what was becoming her customary scowl.

She was still upset—like it was Hope's fault Josiah paid her more attention at dinner. Hope hadn't asked for it. She hadn't even wanted it.

Although, Josiah did seem like a fine person. His handsome looks didn't hurt, either. *If she could just get Abram out of her head.*

But it didn't matter anyway, because for Mary's sake, Hope wouldn't go near Josiah.

She gazed at the overcast skies and watched two blue jays twist and turn through the air. She had heard Abram was back home again, so no doubt he would be at worship. Would he acknowledge her? How should she act? Should she make sure to stand where he would pass?

"Plotting your conquest?" Mary asked.

Hope flinched. "What?"

"Now that Abram's home, you can snatch both him and Josiah." Mary's eyes misted, and she turned away.

"When are you going to forgive me?" asked Hope. "I didn't do anything."

"I'm seventeen." Mary's voice was flat.

"I know how old you are."

"I don't have anyone."

Hope gave a heavy sigh. "Well, neither do I."

Now, she didn't even have Mary. She missed her sister—missed their closeness and their whispered confidences in the middle of the night. She'd done everything she could to bring Mary near again. She'd even done a large portion of her chores over the last week, but nothing swayed Mary's mood.

Mamm came out of the house, followed by Ann and Ruth. *Dat* shut the door and walked down the steps, and every board groaned and creaked under his weight. He was a solid man, and the fact that he doted on Ruth's cooking didn't help his girth.

"Here comes the church wagon!" exclaimed Ann. "And look, Mercy's already in it!" She jumped up and down, waving.

If Mercy was already in the wagon, then…

And sure enough, there he was, sitting next to Josiah. Despite everything, Hope's heart leapt at the sight of him. His posture was easy and relaxed. As the wagon pulled to a stop, his eyes found hers. She averted her gaze and concentrated on boosting Ann into the wagon. *Dat* helped *Mamm* and Ruth. Mary hoisted herself up and Hope followed, sitting as far away from Abram and Josiah as possible. Mary squeezed her way onto the bench right in front of them.

As the horses rounded a bend in the road, Hope dared to glance up. Abram was watching Mercy and Ann with a look of detached amusement, but Josiah's gaze was on her. There was no mistaking the spark of interest in his eyes. He smiled, and she looked away, but not before she saw Mary catch the whole scene. The sadness on her face burned into Hope's skin.

The wind increased, and Hope pressed her hands on her dress to keep it from wafting up. A stray drop of rain plopped on her forehead. And then another fell on her wrist.

"*Ach*," Ruth said, looking at *Dat*. "You were right, Benjamin. Might be a storm coming after all."

"Just a bit of rain," said Abram.

At the rich timbre of his voice, Hope clasped her hands tightly in her lap. The drops stopped, and everyone settled back into quiet chatter for the rest of the drive.

****

During the worship singing, Hope closed her eyes and lost herself in the words of the songs. The hymns in the *Ausbund* always brought her comfort and a feeling of deep contentment.

O Lord Father, we bless thy name, Thy love and thy goodness praise; That thou, O Lord, so graciously have been to us always.

The words were drawn out, each syllable stretched long, every song taking nearly fifteen minutes to sing. Hope relaxed into each verse, her heart warm, and her mind at peace. For those minutes, she forgot about Abram and Josiah and Mary and her hurting ankle.

Mary nudged her, and Hope shifted and turned. "What?" she mouthed.

Hope followed Mary's gaze across the room and saw Josiah watching them, his eyebrows raised. When he noticed them looking, he gave a slow smile. Hope glanced away. Despite herself, she snuck a glance at Abram who was staring at the floor.

Hope tried to lose herself in the song again, but the tension exuding from Mary stopped her. Her sister was perched on the bench like a glass jar about to shatter during canning. Hope scooted closer. "He was probably looking at *you*," she murmured.

Mary squeezed her eyes shut and shook her head; she knew the truth.

Hope squirmed with the knowledge that Josiah had been staring at her. Why couldn't it have been Abram watching her? What was so interesting on the floor anyway? Hope bowed her head. *Why am I thinking of such things during worship? It is not fitting.*

She had to control her thoughts and put them back on God where they belonged. She struggled through the rest of the worship, willing her mind to cooperate.

****

Hope wasn't hungry when it was time for the meal. Instead, she wandered outside through the buggies, trying to regain the peace she'd felt earlier during the hymns. Her ankle ached, but she did her best to ignore it.

"Hope?"

At the sound of his voice, apprehension coursed through her. She turned to see Josiah approach her with his hat in his hand. A tremor near his mouth betrayed his nervousness.

"Hello, Josiah."

"Are you staying for the youth singing this evening?"

She detected a slight catch in his voice.

"I usually do," she answered. She loved the singing, but how could she enjoy herself that night knowing that even though Abram was so close, he might as well be a hundred miles away.

She bit her lip. Josiah wasn't there to talk about Abram.

He continued, "I do have my own horse and buggy, but they're back home with my folks. I'm sure Abram will lend me his if I ask."

Hope tensed, knowing what was coming.

"I was wondering if you'd allow me to give you a ride home tonight. After the singing." He let out his breath in a soft whoosh.

And there it was. Her invitation. She'd been waiting years for such an invitation. Emotion sent her pulses spinning, as the full realization of what this would mean settled in her heart. If she accepted, everyone would assume they were courting. Mary would never speak to her again. Abram would see her as unavailable.

A light sprinkle began to fall, and the soft drops landed on Hope's lashes. She blinked them away and saw Josiah's grip on his hat increase until his knuckles turned white. She didn't want to hurt his feelings, but she knew that accepting him was not God's plan for her.

Josiah shuffled his feet in the dirt. "It's all right. Never mind. Maybe another time."

He put on his hat and turned to leave. As he pivoted, Hope saw Abram a few yards behind him. Abram's broad shoulders were stiff and the look on his face was grim. Had he heard?

Josiah pushed past him and retreated.

Hope couldn't bear the thought of another argument with Abram. Better not to talk at all. She swirled and began running through the increasing rain, dodging around the buggies, toward the Miller's shed. The door hung open and she hurried through, not seeing a rake that had fallen from its hook. She lurched and tripped, and her weak ankle twisted. She collapsed in a heap. Pain shot up her leg, and she grabbed her foot, moaning. Tears splashed down her cheeks, and she squeezed her eyes closed.

"You're hurt. How bad is it?" Abram's voice was thick with concern.

She opened her eyes to him kneeling beside her.

"I'm fine," she said through gritted teeth.

"You're not fine at all."

Abram took off his jacket and folded it into a square. He placed it under her foot.

"I am *too* fine," Hope repeated. Which, of course, she wasn't. She didn't know which hurt worse, her throbbing ankle or her throbbing heart.

Abram squatted back on his haunches and observed her. "So Josiah asked to drive you home after the singing. Are you going with him?"

Hope wiped at her tears and sniffed. His eyes didn't move, and his scrutiny bore into her.

She stifled an inexplicable urge to burst into tears again. All she wanted was this man before her. All she wanted was to admit her love for him. And for him to love her back. But it wasn't to be. She silently prayed for strength and courage. She shook her head, "No, I'm not going with him."

Abram exhaled. "I'll get your *mamm* and *dat*. You'll need your ankle tended to." He stood to go, and she panicked. She couldn't let him leave. She had been wrong to run. They did need to talk.

"Wait." She opened her mouth to say more, but a wave of embarrassment silenced her. She wasn't sure what to say. She wasn't sure what God wanted her to do. Was she taking things into her own hands?

Every inch of her being wanted to know why Abram had gone back to the *Englischers*. Every inch wanted to know why he hadn't been baptized when he'd returned home from *rumspringa*? And was there an *Englisch* girl? Did he want to leave the community?

Each question burned across her face as Abram looked at her.

"You are wondering many things," he said.

His voice was calm, his gaze steady. Hope thought she heard tenderness there, but she didn't dare imagine it. Besides, Abram was right, she needed her *dat* to get her inside, and her *mamm* to tend to her ankle.

But what she really wanted was Abram to take her in his arms—Abram to carry her gently into the Miller house. Her cheeks grew warm with humiliation. She shouldn't think such things.

Abram took her hand in his. "Hope?" he began.

Her eyes grew wide, and her skin started to tingle. "*Jah?*"

"May I take you home tonight after the singing?"

Her breath caught in her throat. And right there, right then, inside the muggy garden shed with her ankle pulsing in pain and tears drying on her cheeks, it was as if the sun had burst forth with dazzling beauty.

Laughter bubbled up inside her. "*Jah*, you can," she whispered and gazed at him with wonder.

Abram helped her up, and she tottered a bit trying to balance on her good foot.

"Lean on me," Abram said. "I'll help you."

His grip was strong and sure as he helped her hobble toward the house.

"There will be plenty of time for all your questions later," he said. "And plenty of time for all my answers."

They both heard the promise in his voice.

Abram's Plan

One

*In everything give thanks: for this is the will of God
in Christ Jesus concerning you.
Thessalonians 5:18 (King James Version)*

At the top of the stairs, Hope paused and sent up a quick prayer of thanks. Abram was coming to supper that day, and the joy of seeing him never got old. Her heart stirred with gladness whenever she gazed into his dark charcoal eyes. Sometimes, when he moved close enough to brush against her, the strength of his arms and the set of his broad shoulders made her downright dizzy. Smiling, she took an extra moment to make sure every stray curl was tucked snugly under her *kapp*.

Satisfied all was in order, Hope began to descend the stairs when *Mamm's* pained voice floated up from the living room below, "*Nee!* Benjamin, no!"

Hope caught her breath. All thoughts of Abram dropped from her mind, and she froze in place, listening.

"How could Priscilla be gone?" *Mamm's* voice twisted with

grief. "She was younger than me."

Dat replied in a low murmur, his words muffled. Fear clenched Hope's heart. *Who was this Priscilla? And what was Dat doing in the house at this time of the morning?*

"I'm sorry," Aunt Ruth's voice joined theirs. "Truly sorry, Elizabeth."

"She had children?" *Mamm* asked.

"Two." *Dat's* heavy tread creaked across the plank floors, and Hope knew he was pacing, something he did only when highly disturbed.

"She was your sister," Ruth said, as if stating a fact from the Almanac.

Hope's eyes widened and a wave of shock gripped her. *Mamm's sister?* That couldn't be right. *Mamm* had two brothers—no sisters.

She grasped the rail, her fingers tightening like wire.

"Someone will have to go," *Dat* said. "You need to go."

"*Nee!*" *Mamm* cried. "I can't. Don't you understand? I can't. She wouldn't want me to."

Dat groaned and the floorboards kept protesting.

Hope pressed her hand to her mouth. She shouldn't be eavesdropping—it wasn't proper. She forced herself away from the stairwell. Then she turned and darted across the hall to the bedroom she shared with her sister. Mary was changing the sheets. Her face was flushed, and unruly blond curls stuck to the nape of her neck.

"*Mamm* has a sister!" Hope blurted out.

Mary's hands ceased moving, and she stared at Hope as if she'd gone daft. "What are you talking about?"

"*And she died!*"

Mary dropped two pillowcases onto the partially made bed and sank onto the folded quilt. "But how can someone die who never existed?"

"She did exist. I heard *Dat* and *Mamm* downstairs."

"You were spying?"

"*Nee*, not on purpose. I heard them. We need to go down and ask."

"You must've misunderstood." Mary blinked, confusion filling her blue eyes. "You're not making sense."

"I know that," Hope answered, tension mounting in her voice. "I'm going downstairs to find out."

Hope turned to go, and Mary hastened to follow. It was quiet below, and Hope wondered if everyone had left. But when they got down, their *mamm* sat slumped in the rocking chair with a stricken look on her face.

When she noticed her oldest daughters gaping at her, she jerked upright, straightened her apron, and headed for the kitchen.

"*Mamm*?" Hope questioned, hurrying after her. "Is everything all right?"

Mamm sniffed. "I'm going to start the stew. Mary, are the beds changed?"

"Almost."

"Then go upstairs and finish." *Mamm* pulled a large pot from the shelf.

Hope stepped close, her voice low. "I heard you, *Mamm*. I didn't mean to, but I heard."

A soft gasp escaped *Mamm's* lips, and her spine seemed to fold in on itself. Hope reached out to grab her, but *Mamm* righted herself and stiffened.

"We have something to discuss with you girls tonight," she said, her voice rigid.

Hope and Mary exchanged looks. Hope knew better than to push the subject; her *mamm* would say no more. They would have to wait.

****

Abram stopped by shortly before supper. When Hope heard his buggy, she ran from the house and stood on the porch to greet him. He grinned and jumped down.

"There's a nice welcome," he said and chuckled as he unhitched his horse. "Walk to the barn with me?"

Hope had to half-run to match his long strides. Abram put his horse in an empty stall and threw in a bit of hay.

"Planning to stay a long while?" Hope teased.

"As long as you'll have me," he answered easily. He set a slower pace back toward the house.

"Something has happened, Abram."

He looked down at her upturned face, framed by soft brown curls that had once again escaped from her *kapp*.

"I thought I detected a limp."

He *would* notice—he was growing to know her well. Ever since she fell off a plow horse at age three, her ankle carried all her stress and worry. It would pain her and sometimes swell enough to make her limp. It made no sense, and it troubled Hope to no end. She could only explain it by comparing it to the way her *grossmammi's* arthritis announced a coming storm.

Abram continued, and his voice registered concern. "What happened? Is someone hurt or ill?"

"*Nee.*" Hope paused. Her news was so recent and unbelievable that she stumbled to put it into words. "I—I think my *mamm* had a sister no one knew existed."

Abram's thick dark brows gathered into a frown. "What do you mean?"

"I—well, I overheard her taking to *Dat*. When I asked her, she said we'd discuss it tonight."

Abram nodded slowly, hesitated, and turned back toward the barn. "Then I shouldn't stay."

Hope's heart sank, yet she knew he was right. This was not

something to discuss outside the family.

"I'd hoped to have more time with you this evening," Abram said. His voice was steady, but she detected a hint of strain.

"What is it?" she asked, catching up to him.

He stopped and faced her. "I hoped to share my plan with you."

Her shoulders tightened, and her mind erupted into a crazy mix of excitement and apprehension. She'd waited long weeks for him to share his plan—ever since he had returned from the *Englisch* world.

Looking at her jumbled expression, he continued. "I'm sorry. I shouldn't have mentioned it on such a day. Forgive me."

She touched his rough hand and felt his warmth tingle up her arm. She pulled away and searched his face. "When?"

The beginnings of a smile tipped the corners of his mouth. "Soon," he promised. His gaze softened at her eagerness.

At that moment, Hope's younger sister Ann bounded up, her blue eyes dancing. Hope saw their puppy Apple in tow as usual. The dog followed Ann as if connected to her with an invisible rope. Apple jumped on Abram's leg and proceeded to tug on his pants.

"*Ach!*" Hope cried. She grabbed up the fluffy puppy and held him out to her sister. "Ann, take your silly Apple elsewhere."

She attempted a firm tone, but Apple's cute face and happy wiggles had won her over weeks ago. She pulled the puppy in for a quick snuggle before Ann took her away.

"You're a softie for the animals," Abram noted.

"Who, me?" Hope questioned, feigning innocence.

"Yes, you." He touched the tip of her nose and smiled. "I'll see myself off."

"Abram," Hope called after him. "Thank you for coming."

He turned to wave. Hope raised her hand in response and watched him disappear into the barn.

Two

During supper, Hope had trouble eating anything. Mostly, she shoved the fresh garden peas and bites of meatloaf from one side of her plate to the other. Much of Mary's food was also untouched. Of the six of them, only Ann seemed to be eating with gusto. But then, only Add didn't know of the coming discussion.

At the end of the meal, Hope and her sisters rose to clear the table, but Ruth stopped them. "Tonight, I clear the dishes," she said, stacking the plates.

Ann grinned. "Thank you, Ruth. *Mamm*, can I go outside and play with Apple?"

Dat coughed and spread his hands on the table. "Not now, Ann. It's time for a family meeting."

Ann's eyebrows rose. "Does this have to do with why Abram didn't stay for supper? Or did we do something wrong?"

"No one did anything wrong," *Dat* said.

Mamm was still, staring at the wall opposite her.

"We've had news." *Dat* took a folded envelope from beneath his napkin. "Your *mamm's* sister has recently died."

Ann's gaze flew to *Mamm*. "What sister? You had a sister?"

Dat gave her a firm look and continued. "Her name was Priscilla, and we've only just received word." He pulled papers from the envelope and laid them on the table. "She was killed recently in a car accident."

"But *Mamm*, what sister? Was she our aunt then?" Ann's blue eyes stretched wide.

"Ann, let me finish. There are children. Two. A boy, Jack, who is fourteen. And a girl, Sally, who is sixteen. We are going to fetch them this weekend."

Hope's mouth dropped open. "They're coming here to live?"

Dat stood and leaned over the table. "Hope, they've lost their *mamm*. We must take them in. They're kin."

"That's not what I meant, *Dat*. I just don't understand. What about their own father? And how do we have cousins we know nothing about?" Hope's mind was still spinning.

Mamm stood, looking so shaky, Hope half-expected her to collapse to the floor. "Tell them all, Benjamin."

With halting steps, *Mamm* made her way to the stairs and began to climb, leaning heavily on the railing. She looked so sad, so lost, so not like their mother. Tears gathered in Hope's throat, making it hard to breathe.

Dat sank back into his chair at the head of the table. "Priscilla made her decision long ago. She rejected our way of life and left."

"She was placed on *bann*?" Mary asked.

If Priscilla was placed on *bann* and fled, everything would make more sense. In that case, no one would have been eager to speak of her.

Dat inhaled sharply. "She left and never returned. She never tried to communicate with any of the family. It was as if she no longer existed."

"Why didn't *Mamm* tell us about her?" Hope asked.

Dat stared up the empty staircase and then back at them. "It wasn't easy on your *mamm*. She and Priscilla had been close until…"

Hope leaned across the table. "Until what?"

"There were problems. Your *mamm* didn't know—she didn't understand. For all their closeness, Priscilla never let on." *Dat's* eyes glazed over as if lost in the past.

"Let on to what?" Ann finally asked.

Dat flinched and focused back on his daughters.

"It was a courting issue. The details aren't important. Priscilla left and never contacted anyone again. We didn't know where she was. We didn't know she had children. But now she's gone, and the children have no one but us."

"Where are they now?" Hope couldn't imagine having no one left but strangers for family.

"We are hiring a van to take us to Indianapolis. From there, we will take a bus to Ohio. The children are in Ohio staying with a local pastor. They're waiting for us."

"When do you leave?" asked Mary.

"Tomorrow."

The dining room became silent. Hope looked at her sisters. She observed them struggle to understand the news along with her. Ruth stood erect in the kitchen doorframe, watching all of them, her face a study of grief and guilt. Hope wondered why it should have such an effect on her. As *Dat's* sister, had Ruth known Priscilla well? And had something happened between them, too?

Ruth shuddered and became all business again. "We'll need to rearrange the bedrooms. Ann, you'll move in with me. Hope and Mary, Sally will have to fit in with you. Jack will have Ann's room."

The three girls nodded. A numbness spread over Hope. How could her mother have never mentioned a sister? *Bann* or not, runaway or not, it didn't seem possible.

But one thing she knew for sure: all their lives were about to change.

****

The next day was Tuesday. As usual, Hope found an excuse to go to the Feed & Supply store as Abram always stopped there on Tuesday mornings. She was eager to talk with him—eager to share the story of her unknown cousins.

But more than that, she was eager to know his plan. She speculated about whether he'd share it with her right there in the dusty parking lot. Chocolate nudged Hope's shoulder, and she batted at the flies hovering around the mare's ears.

"Need a little help, girl?" she laughed, stroking the horse's nose.

The spices—her excuse this time for the trip in—lay neatly wrapped on the front seat of her buggy. She felt a bit silly waiting next to Chocolate. If the Troyers peered outside, they'd come out to ask if something was wrong. And what would she say? *Ach, I'm only hoping to catch a glimpse of Abram today?*

Just as she was despairing her trip was in vain, she saw the Lambright's buggy and road horse, Sprint, trotting in her crooked way down the road. Abram made a fine picture, sitting tall, driving the old mare with such ease. She admired him until her cheeks flushed. When he drew near, she busied herself fussing with Chocolate's harness.

"Hope!" Abram called. He jumped down and walked to where she stood.

"Hello, Abram."

"How did it go last evening?" There was concern in his eyes.

"It was true. *Mamm* did have a sister. She left many years ago." Hope's voice was soft, and she proceeded to tell him all she knew. She watched his face register all she shared. Having his full attention was addictive, and when she finished, she wished she had more to say.

"So, you'll have more in the household now."

She nodded.

The sun went behind a thin gray cloud and a breeze stirred. A wagon pulled into the lot, and both Hope and Abram nodded to the Schrock family.

Abram looked off to a grassy area by the side of the store where a faded wooden bench rested under a sprawling maple tree. "Can you sit a spell?" he asked.

Her smile broadened. "*Jah. Mamm* won't expect me home for a while."

Abram returned to his buggy to pat Sprint's nose and pull a handful of grain from a small bag under the buggy seat. Sprint snorted and slurped up the treat with her fleshy lips. Abram and Hope walked over to the bench, and Hope carefully sat a good distance from him, not wanting to appear too familiar in public.

"So I finally get to hear it? Your plan?" Her voice cracked with eagerness.

He grinned. "You finally get to hear it."

He rubbed his hands down his thighs as if wiping away sweat. She waited.

"I'm buying the old Miller farm."

Hope was incredulous. "What? The Millers are leaving?"

"*Nee*, not those Millers. The *old* Miller place. The farm east of the schoolhouse."

And then she remembered. It was a fair piece of acreage, but the house was in bad shape, though the oversized barn had always looked solid.

"I know the place. You're buying it?"

She couldn't hide her surprise. Everyone in the community recognized that the last few years had been hard on the Lambright family. She knew every spare cent had gone to making ends meet. How could Abram possibly have the money to buy the Miller place?

And then realization dawned. Her eyes grew wide with wonder. "Your *rumspringa*. You were earning money. And when you went back—"

Abram nodded, and a pleased half-smile played on his face.

"But, I thought you gave all your money to your *dat*…"

"I tried, but he wouldn't take it. He finally agreed to take a portion." Abram took off his hat and fingered the wide straw brim.

Hope watched his calloused hands. He was a hard worker. Harder than she had known. Abram was one of the few Amish teens who actually left the area during *rumspringa*. When he didn't come back for months, most folks assumed he was playing hard. Why else would he have stayed away for such long stretches?

"But why didn't you tell me? Why didn't you tell everyone?"

Abram sighed and clapped his hat on his knees as if shaking off dust. "Originally, I only wanted to earn money for *Dat*. I didn't announce it because he was ashamed to be in such a bad way."

"But it happens, Abram. It could happen to anyone."

He held up his hand. "But it didn't happen to anyone. It happened to *Dat*. To us, our family. I felt for him. So I kept quiet. Then when he refused to take all my money, my ideas changed. Why not save for a farm of my own? I know a lot of Amish work for others, but I want to work for myself, for my own family."

He looked at her as if testing her response then continued. "I thought that I could save up enough for a down payment. The old Miller place had gone back to the bank. The house on the property was a wreck. Turns out, the bank was eager to part with it."

"You already went to the bank?" She marveled, for to her mind, bank business in the *Englisch* world was confusing at best.

"I'm twenty, Hope. Nearly twenty-one. Old enough."

"To buy a place?"

"My uncle helped. And he signed the loan with me."

Hope closed her lips and stared at him. Her mind whirled to organize all his revelations. "But you didn't accept baptism when you returned." That fact had caused her more worry than she cared to admit. "I thought you wanted to leave the faith."

He reached over and clasped her small hand in his strong one. His eyes were pained.

"I didn't have enough money. I knew I'd need to go back and work for Robby's father again."

"Which is why you left the second time."

He nodded. "I didn't want to be baptized into the church and then disappear. Once I'm baptized, I will stay. For good."

She shook her head slowly as if clearing her thoughts. "I thought you wanted to leave," she said again, this time in a whisper.

He squeezed her hand and then let go when the Schrocks emerged from the store. The Schrock children glanced over, smiled, and then piled into their wagon.

"Hope," Abram said, his voice low.

"*Jah?*"

"I'm going to be baptized now."

"No more leaving?"

"No more leaving." He smiled at her and set his hat on the bench. "And there's another part to my plan."

Her breath caught in her throat, and her skin began to tingle.

He inhaled deeply. "I want you to marry me."

A soft gasp escaped Hope's mouth, and she suddenly felt dizzy. Abram's face registered alarm. "Are you all right, Hope? Did I speak out of turn?" He moved closer. "It's just that I love you, Hope."

Joy coursed through her, and it was a moment before she could speak. Tears welled, and her voice was soft as a newborn chick, "Abram. Abram, *jah*. Of course, I will marry you."

They looked at each other. A sparrow landed in the tree above them and chirped its melodious call, and they both burst into laughter.

"And, Abram, I love you, too."

Relief and contentment covered his face. "We will keep it silent for now, *jah*? In the traditional way. After the harvest, we will tell the others and be published at the proper time."

Hope nodded. She couldn't stop nodding. Everything within her swelled with happiness and gratitude.

Now she knew Abram's plan.

And it revolved around her.

Three

The following day, Hope worked to keep her news quiet. She gathered eggs and sang to the hens. She picked zucchini and greeted every plant in the vast garden with a grin. She swept the porch with a light step. She hummed when she went down to the root cellar for more flour.

After lunch, Mary stared at her with consternation. "I don't know why you're so happy about unknown cousins coming. They're going to upset everything."

Aunt Ruth frowned at Mary from across the table. "Mary, keep still. Your *mamm* is going to need everyone's help and kindness. We all need to ask for the good Lord's grace and patience."

Mary scowled.

"When will they be here?" Ann asked, leaning down to pet Apple, who was yipping under the table.

"*Mamm* would have a fit if she knew that dog was inside during a meal," Mary scolded.

Ruth stood and collected the serving dishes. "They'll be home tonight. Are the beds ready?"

"They're ready," Hope said. She forced a serious look to her face, but it took effort. It took effort to keep from bursting into joyful giggles. It took effort to remain indoors at all. What she wanted to do was run through the cornfields and sing about her precious love to the heavens.

It was nearly bedtime when they heard the van pull up to their house. Hope grabbed up the oil lantern, and the four of them filed out to the porch. The sky was speckled with stars, and the air was cool and fresh. Fireflies dotted the ground and swirled close to the bushes out front.

The passenger door of the white van opened and *Dat* and *Mamm* emerged. Alone.

Ann ran down the steps. "Where are they? Where are our cousins?"

Mamm patted her shoulder and trudged up to the front door. Fatigue rolled off her in waves.

"Elizabeth?" Ruth questioned, touching *Mamm's* arm as she passed.

"Let's go inside," *Dat* said and shepherded them to the dining room. Hope set the lantern in the middle of the table. "Sit down, everyone," *Dat* said.

They sat.

"It's been a long day. We met the children. The pastor they're staying with is a good man."

"But I thought they—" Ann interrupted.

Dat held up his rough, weathered hand. His face was grim and the wrinkles around his mouth were pronounced. "Please, Ann, let me continue. The children are finishing up some special summer session. Something to do with their school. It will continue until well into August. The pastor told us it is a coveted program, and the children worked hard to be placed in it."

"Is that why they didn't come? So they could finish the program? Will they stay with the pastor's family until it's over?" Hope asked.

"*Nee*," *Mamm* said. She shifted her weight with a look of complete discomfort, and her hands were clasped so tightly together on the table, her knuckles had gone white. "We can't ask a stranger to keep our own."

"Then why didn't you bring them home?" Mary asked.

"Your *mamm* thought it best not to break them away yet. They are deeply upset. We thought if they were allowed to finish their special program, they would feel better about moving here. We prayed and feel it is what *Gott* would have us do," *Dat* said.

"But if they don't stay with the pastor, will they stay by themselves?" Ann asked.

"*Nee.*"

Hope looked at her mother and pity washed over her at the tortured look in her eyes.

"What is your plan then?" Ruth asked.

Dat cleared his throat. "Hope will go to Ohio to stay with them. When the session is over, they will come home together."

Hope's heart lurched, and she jumped off the bench. "*Nee!* I can't go."

How could she be away from Abram so long? After he'd finally declared himself? She simply couldn't leave him. And there wasn't all that much time until they would be published in October, and their intentions would be made public. After that, it would be a whirlwind until the wedding a couple weeks later.

Everyone's eyes stretched wide as they stared at her. It was unheard of to defy *Dat* in such a way. Hope's face burned red, and she sank back to the bench.

"Sorry, *Dat*," she murmured, her stomach rising to her throat. She quickly sent up a silent prayer. *Gott, please help me. I'm sorry for being disrespectful, but please, please, please, don't make me leave Abram.*

"I will go," Ruth said.

Hope clasped her chest. "Thank you, Ruth." *And thank you, Gott.* She turned hopeful eyes to her father.

His gaze focused on his eldest daughter. "I don't understand your hesitation, Hope, but I'm sorry. It has been decided."

Ruth leaned forward. "Benjamin, send me. There is no reason for Hope to go. I am fully capable of taking care of the children."

Dat's gaze darted to *Mamm* before answering. His voice was pained. "*Nee*, Ruth. Elizabeth wants Hope to do it. You understand why."

Hope struggled to hide her confusion. "But *Dat*, I don't—"

Ruth abruptly left the room. Hope watched her go, wondering at the look of shame on her face. There had to be much more to this story than was being told.

****

Hope expected Abram to feel the same despair she felt at the news, but she was mistaken.

"It is *Gott's* will, Hope. He knows what is best. Besides, I have much work to do on the house. I will get it done fast, *jah*? Without you to distract me?" His eyes were warm and teasing on hers.

She wished she could be so accepting, but the thought of being away from Abram so long brought only pain to her heart.

He gave her a quick, fierce hug, and she felt his strength and love.

"We will be together soon," he assured her. "And when you return, we will tell both families of our plan."

She wanted to cling to him, but she knew it wasn't fitting, nor would it make leaving him any easier.

"You will write?" she asked.

"I will write." He tilted his head and gave her an irresistible grin.

His lean frame and firm features imprinted themselves on her mind. She closed her eyes and took a slow breath. It would be all right. God would give her strength to leave this precious man.

When she opened her eyes again, he was gone.

****

Hope clasped the tattered suitcase she had borrowed from Ruth as if it would fly away. She climbed into the van and peered through the window at her family. They stood in a row on the porch, waving her off. Except for Ann, their waves were half-hearted and their expressions solemn. The driver glanced at Hope from the rearview mirror.

"You ready, miss?"

She nodded. She hadn't been in a van all that often and almost never alone. Many Amish went on long road trips, visiting kin throughout the Midwest and East. But not her family. Five times, they had gone to visit kin in a community sixty miles away, and she remembered well her excitement. But this was different. It would take a couple hours to get to Indianapolis, and then there would be three more hours by bus to Ohio.

Abram would be out in his father's fields now, perspiring in the heat, helping his *dat* with the crops. And later, when he was bone-tired, he would go to his own farm, *their* farm, and work hours longer. Readying their new home. Hope treasured her secret engagement in her heart and prayed all would go favorably while she was away.

She was the only passenger in the van that morning, and she knew her father had paid dearly for the ride. She leaned her forehead against the window and watched the farmland streak by.

"You all right, miss?" the driver asked, glancing over his shoulder. "You're not carsick, are you?"

"*Nee*, sir. I'm fine."

The ride was smooth, much smoother than the buggy, and they seemed to fly down the road. Her thoughts drifted to her new cousins. How would they be feeling having just lost their mother? Hope couldn't imagine life without her *mamm*. She couldn't imagine getting up in the morning and not seeing *Mamm* bustling about the kitchen—not seeing *Mamm* sitting, bending over her mending and quilt making—not seeing *Mamm* kneeling in her flower garden.

Her eyes welled with tears, and she sent up a silent prayer. *Gott, please help my new cousins and forgive me for my earlier selfishness. I am ashamed of my self-seeking thoughts and actions. Thank you for the compassion and love you are giving me for my kin. Help me to be a comfort to them.*

Hope folded her hands on her lap and relaxed into the seat. Speaking with God often calmed her and restored her sense of balance.

She decided right then that she would work hard to be the best cousin and caretaker she could be for both Sally and Jack. She repeated the names softly to herself. *Sally and Jack.* She'd never known anyone by those particular names.

Now she would.

Four

In Ohio, the bus wheezed to a stop, and Hope stirred, realizing she had been asleep for the last hour or so. She'd meant to memorize every detail of the trip to share with her two sisters and Abram. She sat up straight, embarrassed to have fallen asleep in the middle of the day. Was this how she was going to act in the *Englisch* world? Like a lazy girl?

Dat had told her she would be picked up by the pastor who would then drive her to meet Sally and Jake. Swallowing her trepidation, she scanned the crowd even though she had no idea what the pastor looked like.

She spotted a kindly-looking man craning his head, checking as each passenger disembarked. Their eyes met, and he smiled.

"Hope? Hope Lehman?" he called out.

Hope guessed his age to be a bit younger than her parents. He was dressed casually, in jeans and a tucked-in shirt and belt. She breathed deeply. Adjusting to *Englisch* clothing was the least of her worries.

He approached her with his hand extended. Hope stared at his outstretched fingers and then slipped her hand in his for a gentle shake. It felt odd to take a stranger's hand, but she didn't want to appear unfriendly.

"*Jah*, I'm Hope Lehman," she said with a shy smile.

"I'm Pastor Rankin. Sally and Jack are waiting for you back at the house. They're still struggling with the situation. I thought it best if you met them there." He looked at her small suitcase. "Are the rest of your things in the storage compartment under the bus? I can get them for you."

"The rest of my things?" Hope repeated. "*Nee*, this is all I have."

His eyebrows rose, but he said nothing. "Come then. You must be tired."

He led her to an old blue truck with dents streaming down its left side. Patches of rust spotted the bottom of the passenger door.

"Looks bad, but runs like a dream," Pastor Rankin said with a grin.

Hope climbed in, and they took off. The trip from the bus station was short. In a few minutes, Pastor Rankin pulled the clattering truck to the curb in front of a small yellow house. It was only one story, and the front was bordered by a thick row of bushes. Roses flanked both sides of the small porch, and Hope saw that they needed tending; rose hips were already forming where the blooms had faded.

Pastor Rankin turned off the engine and grabbed her suitcase from behind the seat. They got out and walked up the short sidewalk to the front door.

Hope's heart beat wildly, and she prayed her new cousins wouldn't hear it. Pastor Rankin leaned in front of her to open the door. Hope stepped inside the chilly entrance. She heard a soft hum and knew it was an air conditioner. She shivered and walked through to a small living room. On the couch in front of her sat Sally and Jack, both perched like tired roosters on a fence. Sally's thin brown hair hung loosely over her shoulders, and she looked as if a mere breeze would blow her away. She wore heavy eye make-up, and Hope had the fleeting thought of the raccoon that used to steal Apple's dog food.

Jack's face was shadowed and his slumping shoulders brought pain to Hope's heart.

"Sally, Jack, this is your cousin, Hope," Pastor Rankin said.

Sally balanced the cell phone she'd been holding on the arm of the couch. She attempted a smile, but it appeared more like a grimace.

"Hello, Sally," Hope said. She turned to Jack. "Hello, Jack."

Pastor Rankin bustled over to a bookshelf and picked up a piece of paper. "I wrote down everything I thought you might want to know." He pointed to the bottom of the page. "These are my phone numbers—my cell, my house, and the church office. You call if you need anything. Anything at all. Do you have money?"

"*Dat* gave me some money," Hope said.

Pastor Rankin motioned her into the kitchen with a nod. He lowered his voice. "Your aunt didn't have much. As I told your parents, I worked with her lawyer. Rent here is paid through August, which should give you plenty of time. Me and the missus can help you sell all the furniture. A good yard sale ought to do it, and luckily, it's still the season for them. Priscilla did have some money in her checking account which will help with groceries and such. Sally's name is also on the account, so you'll have no problem getting the money."

Pastor Rankin studied her face and lowered his voice further. "One more thing. There is no father—he deserted them years ago. Priscilla never spoke of him after he ran off, and we respected her on that. He had no family we know of. Anyway, your mother was the one listed for the kids. I shared this with your parents but wanted to be sure you knew."

Hope's mind spun. How was she to handle all of this?

He tilted his head, and his eyes were sad. "I'm sorry. You're tired, and I'm overstaying. My missus accuses me of that all the time. Let's go back to the children."

Pastor Rankin returned to the living room and leaned down to pat Jack's head. "These are good kids. Great kids, as a matter of fact. The missus and I loved having them. But we know it's better to be with family. Nothing's better than family. Oh, Hope, the missus made a casserole, and we stocked the fridge. You can heat the casserole in the micro. Shouldn't take long."

He looked at her cousins. "You all right, kids? You need anything else?"

Sally's eyes were moist, but she shook her head. Jack stared at the floor.

"All right then," Pastor Rankin said. "I'll be off. Nice to meet you, Hope. Perhaps you'll want to come to dinner after church this Sunday."

Hope was so overwhelmed, all she could do was nod. With a final glance around the room, Pastor Rankin smiled and left, leaving them in what felt like a huge vacuum.

Hope cleared her throat. "Hello again." She walked to a padded rocking chair next to the window and sat facing them. "I'm glad to meet you."

She smoothed her dress over her knees.

"Are you going to dress like that the whole time?" Sally asked.

"*Jah.* They're my clothes. And are you going to dress like that?" she asked, trying to make a joke.

Neither of them laughed. A patch of red moved up Hope's neck.

"*Ach,* that wasn't funny. I'm sorry. But mostly, I'm sorry about your mother. Truly sorry."

The girl looked strangely familiar, but Hope couldn't imagine why. Then it dawned on her: Sally looked like *Mamm,* especially around the mouth. She had the same full lower lip and the same slight dimple on the right side. The resemblance gave Hope an eerie sensation.

"I'll show you to your room," Sally said. She got up and Hope followed her down a narrow hallway. Sally pushed open the last door. "This was Mom's room. We didn't know where else to put you even though it doesn't seem right that you should sleep here."

Hope glanced around the room, noting it was still full of

personal belongings. Books lined a shelf above the bed. Glass figurines were scattered across the dresser. The closet door was open and clothing hung neatly above a collection of shoes paired up on the floor. Hope glanced at the bed. How could she sleep in a dead person's bed? Then she scolded herself for having such thoughts when the girl beside her was in such obvious pain.

"It will be fine," she said quietly. She set her suitcase on the bed and turned to Sally. "Are you hungry?"

Sally shrugged, her thin shoulders clearly outlined under her shirt.

Hope remembered how she felt when her *grossmammi* had passed away—like she would never be hungry again. "I'll warm the casserole for you. Then you can eat if you want."

She opened her suitcase and removed her apron. Tying it in place made her feel better, more comfortable. The two of them went to the kitchen and Hope removed a glass dish full of sliced potatoes, cheese, and hamburger from the refrigerator.

"Do you even know what a microwave is?" Sally asked. "You don't have lights, right? I'll be living in the stone age."

Hope swallowed. "I do know what a microwave is, but why don't you show me how to use it?" Her voice was gentle, but she took a deep breath and prayed for wisdom.

****

Hope had breakfast ready by five-thirty the next morning. She'd found eggs to scramble and sausage to fry. She'd looked for potatoes, but finding none, she settled instead on setting out some bread and butter. She'd neglected to find out when her cousins needed to catch the school bus Sally had mentioned the night before.

The house was still and so quiet, Hope felt almost spooked. She looked around for something to keep herself from being idle, but could find nothing to do. She was unsure whether she should rouse her cousins and call them in for breakfast.

A moan caught her attention, and she turned to see Sally shuffle into the kitchen wearing loose pants and an even looser shirt.

"Why are you up so early?" Sally asked.

"At home, we always have breakfast ready early. There is so much to do in the fields and the animals need tending to, and —" she stopped at the bewildered look on Sally's face. "I'm sorry. I'm talking too much."

Sally plopped down on one of the metal chairs around the kitchen table. "I'm half Amish," she stated as if reporting the weather.

Hope sat across from her. "*Jah*, you are."

"Mom wouldn't talk about it."

Hope kept silent.

"I think Mom was ashamed. I hoped that maybe when I got older, she'd tell me more. But now —" Sally's voice caught, and she pressed her lips together.

There were paper napkins on the table and Hope offered her one. Sally grabbed it and wadded it up into her fist.

"I guess I'll find out about it now," she said. "Whether I like it or not."

"*Jah*."

"Jack hardly talks." Sally looked at Hope through tears. "He used to blabber all day. It was annoying. So annoying. I hassled him about it constantly." She took a big breath.

Hope waited, and when Sally said no more, asked, "Do you want some eggs?"

"I heard Amish kids don't go to school."

"We do. But only through the eighth grade."

Sally shook her head, and her fist tightened. "So, what are Jack and I supposed to do?"

Hope reached out and put her soft hand over her cousin's clenched one. Sally shook it off, and Hope sighed.

"There is a high school in Hollybrook. You can go there."

It would be a chore to take them into town each day. She supposed they could ride in on bicycles, or maybe a school bus would fetch them. She wasn't sure how the system worked.

Sally smoothed out the napkin and then blew her nose. "Jack and I got in the gifted program this summer. Mom was proud." Again, her voice caught.

Hope wasn't sure what a gifted program was, but she nodded.

"It's not as great as we thought. The teacher who was supposed to be in charge went and got pregnant, and now she's on bed rest so they put Mr. Shane in charge. He's pretty much a whack job."

Sally went to the stove and dished herself some eggs.

"I can get that for you," Hope said, jumping up from the table.

"Don't bother. I've got it." Sally returned and sank into her chair. She took a couple small bites. "Aren't you going to eat?"

"*Jah.* I'll join you. Should we get Jack up?"

"I don't want to move away from my friends," Sally said and sucked in her breath. "I don't want to live backwards with no one I even know."

Hope's throat ached for this girl in front of her. "I'm sorry."

"I only insisted we stay until the program was over because I don't want to leave. Jack is really upset. I'm not sure I'm enough for him." Her words were edged in fear.

Hope wasn't accustomed to someone she hardly knew bearing her heart with such raw emotion.

"You don't have to do it alone." Hope set her eggs aside. "You have *Mamm* and *Dat* and Ruth, and all of us. We'll help you."

Sally pushed her plate to the middle of the table. She sniffed and wiped her nose with the wadded-up napkin. "Can I try it on?" she asked.

"Try what on?"

"Your hat? Or your *kapp*, I mean. I've done research."

Hope's eyebrows rose. This girl opposite her was full of surprises. She slipped off her *kapp* and held it out.

Sally placed it on the top of her tousled hair. "How do I look?"

Hope thought her *kapp* looked strangely at home on Sally's head, but she wasn't sure that's what Sally wanted to hear.

Sally took the covering off and fingered it gingerly.

"Sally, you don't have to dress Amish when you live with us. You can wear your *Englisch* clothes." Hope's voice was soft.

Sally's eyes welled up. "But everything else. What about everything else? I'm losing my whole life." Her voice rose, and her cheeks grew flushed. "Sorry. I know you're trying to be nice."

Hope's heart went out to this girl who was searching for a new place to belong.

Sally handed the *kapp* back to Hope. "I've wondered for a long time about everything Amish. I wondered, but I didn't think I'd have to live it."

She coughed and glanced at the clock on the stove. "Now it is time to get Jack up, or we'll miss the bus."

Five

Two weeks later, Hope stood in the middle of the living room and glanced around. Everything was tidy. She'd long ago washed the dishes and put everything away in the kitchen. The laundry was done. Dinner was partially prepared. She considered fetching the quilt pieces she'd stuck in her suitcase almost as an afterthought. She hadn't brought enough for a full quilt, but she did bring enough to get a good start.

Restlessness filled her. Perhaps she should start packing up the house. There were some boxes in the garage. She could use them. But then, Pastor Rankin said they'd have a yard sale. And what would Sally and Jack want to bring to Indiana? She could hardly make those decisions for them, nor would they welcome her sorting through their rooms.

She walked through the kitchen and stepped outside onto a small patio. The entire yard was barely as big as their chicken coop back home. Hope took a deep breath, relishing the outside air. Inside, the air-conditioned coolness felt unnatural. She admitted that she welcomed a fan during the hottest months, but the air conditioning was too much. She considered turning it off that morning when Sally and Jack had left, but she'd done that once before and Sally hadn't liked it.

A robin landed in the dirt near a small clump of daisies and set about poking for worms. Hope smiled and a pang of yearning for home swirled through her heart.

Abram, she whispered, *what are you doing right now? Are your morning chores finished? How is the house coming? I miss you. I miss you dearly.*

She pulled his letter from the waistband of her apron and read it for the hundredth time. She was pleased that he'd written so soon. It hadn't taken long for his letter to arrive. Of course, she'd written back immediately, and Sally had given her a stamp and shown her how to balance the letter half-in and half-out of the mail slot in the door. The postman had whisked it away that very afternoon

Hope closed her eyes and fought the homesickness. *Dear Gott, give me a grateful heart. Give me contentment. I miss my family so much. I miss Abram so much. Help me to be what my cousins need, and help me to do my service here in a way that pleases you.*

Hope tried with all her heart to mean it. She felt compassion and even a growing love for her cousins, but she couldn't erase the desire for her time there to be over.

Her stay had been going fairly well. Sally seemed resigned to the massive changes in her life. Hope worried that an explosion might be building, but she had no idea how to help Sally beyond loving her and praying for her. And pray she did. Morning, noon, and night. Sally did appear relieved to confide in Hope, and day by day, they were growing closer. But still, Hope couldn't stifle the fear that too much was brewing deep inside Sally—a place where neither she nor Sally could find it.

Jack remained sullen. His pained face grew darker every day. He hardly spoke, and Hope worried about him constantly. She tried to break through his walls, but had no real success.

Hope turned and went back into the house just in time to hear the squeak of the mail slot. She hurried across the room, hoping against hope there would be another letter from Abram. She bent to pick up the mail and saw Mary's script on an envelope.

She tore it open and began reading.

Our Hope, We miss you so much. I have to admit I'm a bit jealous of you having such an adventure, while I'm here doing most of your chores plus my own. Mamm and Dat send their love. Please don't worry, but I

have to share some news. Abram is really okay—

Hope's heart lurched to her throat, and her eyes grew wide.

—but he broke his leg. Pretty bad. There was an accident with his road horse. I'm sorry I don't know more. I asked his sister Mercy, and she said that the doctor hoped it would be fine in a couple months. There's only a small chance some damage will be permanent. Abram can't work right now. I'm sure he'll write and explain everything, but I wanted to make sure you knew. Even though the two of you have had misunderstandings, I know you're still sweet on him. Your sister, Mary.

Hope sank to the couch and read the letter again. And then again.

A broken leg? An accident with his road horse? Sprint? Abram was skilled with animals. What had happened? If he couldn't work, how would he help bring in the harvest?

And how would he be able to work on their house?

Hope's shoulders slumped. There would be no time. Would they have to postpone the wedding?

Hope shook her head. *Nee. Nee.* She was being silly. They could still be married. Many newlywed couples lived with their parents until they got established. *Jah,* they could do that. She was sure *Dat* and *Mamm* would let them.

Her thoughts ground to a halt.

Sally and Jack were moving in. Where would she and Abram possibly fit into the house? There wasn't enough room.

They could stay with Abram's family. *Of course.* That would work. But even as she put words to the thought, she knew Abram would never agree. The last years had been hard on his family. More than hard. He'd never add to their burden by bringing another person into the house, even if it was his wife.

She jumped off the couch and began to pace. Her solid black shoes thumped across the floor as she moved from the living room to the kitchen and back. She could help get the house ready. She was strong and able. She could clean and patch walls and paint and work in the yard. And she could even help Abram with the bigger jobs. She could hand him boards and tools and...

Her heart lifted. Of course, she could. She wasn't helpless. Not by any means.

She stopped short. What was she thinking? She wasn't even in Hollybrook. She was here in Ohio where she would be for another few weeks.

She could hardly help Abram long distance.

And her Abram was *hurt*. She walked back to the bedroom and perched on the edge of the bed. Would he be all right? Would his leg heal completely?

If they couldn't get married this wedding season, they could get married the following year. And some even married out of season; although, *Dat* would probably never agree to it. She tried to convince herself that postponement wouldn't matter, but a heavy sadness enveloped her. More than anything in her life, she wanted to marry Abram. She yearned to build a life with him—to have a family with him. Waiting another year was unthinkable.

She folded her hands on top of the letter. All she wanted to do was go home. She bowed her head to pray.

****

Sally stood with her hand on the door knob, ready to leave the house for the bus. Jack was behind her, his backpack hanging off his shoulder.

"Are you going to tell us what's wrong?" Sally snapped.

"What do you mean?" Hope asked.

"You've been weird."

"Sally, let's go," Jack said. They were his first words of the day, and Hope was surprised to hear them at all.

Sally glared at him then turned her attention back to Hope. "Did you fall or something? Because this morning, it seems like you're limping."

She strode to where Hope stood at the kitchen door.

"Something's wrong. You're not the same."

Hope sighed. She'd done her best to act normally since she got the news of Abram's accident. She'd prayed continually that his leg would heal properly. She'd prayed for grace and joy at staying in Ohio and serving her cousins.

Evidently, she hadn't done a very good job of concealing her heart.

Sally frowned. "Are you going to tell us?"

Jack stood next to the door, a black look on his face.

"I had news from home," Hope finally admitted.

Sally stiffened. "And?"

"My friend Abram was in an accident. He broke his leg. The doctor isn't sure if it will heal right."

"Your friend?"

Hope nodded.

Sally grimaced and then shook her head. She studied Hope's face. "I'm sixteen, Hope. And not stupid. He's more than a friend, isn't he?"

Hope cast her eyes downward.

"Okay. I get it. And you're stuck here with us, right?"

Hope shook her head. "*Nee, nee*, Sally. I'm glad to be here with you. You're family."

Sally said nothing. Her brows drew together, and for a moment it looked like she might cry. Or yell. Hope wasn't sure which.

Instead, Sally turned and walked back to the door. "Come on, Jack," she said.

She opened the door, and they left without another word. Hope watched them go with a sense of failure rising in her chest. She shouldn't have said anything. She should have kept her big mouth closed.

****

The day dragged on. Hope scrubbed the kitchen floor, even though it didn't need it. She swept the front porch and the back patio. Twice. She wrote an encouraging letter to Abram, assuring him again that of course his leg would heal up good and proper. She stitched a few quilt pieces. And she made the best dinner possible, even managing to gather all the ingredients for a sugar cream pie.

When the front door opened, the house smelled of stew and pie and homemade biscuits.

"Wow, it smells great in here," Sally exclaimed.

Hope was relieved to see that both of them seemed in better spirits than when they'd left that morning.

"Did you make a pie?" Sally asked.

"Sugar cream. It's my specialty," Hope said. She bustled to the kitchen, getting the dishes on the table.

"Can we talk to you?" Sally asked, her tone serious.

Hope stopped moving and turned to examine Sally's face. Maybe things hadn't improved after all. She followed her back into the living room. Sally sat on the couch and patted the spot beside her for Jack. With a sigh of reluctance, Jack sat. Hope sank into the rocking chair opposite them.

"Can you call your dad? Or do you have to write him?"

Hope's brows rose. *What was this about?* "Well, writing is easier. But I could call the phone shanty outside of Feed & Supply and someone would probably answer. But why? What's wrong?"

Sally had never looked so thin and vulnerable. Hope couldn't imagine what she was thinking.

"Jack and I were talking."

Hope waited for her to continue.

"The gifted program. It's been hard." Sally looked at her brother, and he bit his lower lip. "Everybody stares at us, like

they're waiting for us to cry or act weird or have a nervous
breakdown. They treat us like we're sick or something. I expected it
at first. I mean it only made sense right after it happened. But now?
Even my two best friends are acting like jerks. No offense. I know
they don't mean to. And they know I'm leaving. So, I guess they're
cutting their losses."

She inhaled deeply and went on, "I thought it would stop. But
it hasn't. And the teacher has no clue. In fact, the teacher is pretty
much a fool."

"I'm so sorry," Hope said.

"So I … I mean Jack and me, well, we might as well go to
Hollybrook now."

Hope's lips parted. She felt a flutter in her belly. "What? Now?
Are you serious?"

"We have to go anyway," Sally said. She shrugged like it meant
nothing, but her eyes betrayed her apprehension.

"Is this because of what I told you about Abram?" Hope asked.

Sally lifted her chin. "Maybe a little."

Tears of gratitude clouded Hope's eyes. The pure sweetness of
her gesture left her speechless.

Sally shoulders drooped, and her words rushed out in a torrent.
"I know you want to go home, and it's not good anymore here,
Hope. I hate it. Mom is gone. Jack won't talk. Mom is gone, Hope.
Gone."

Her words ended in a sob. Hope sprang from her chair and
rushed to her. She put her arms around Sally's shaking body and
held tight.

"It's going to be okay, Sally. Truly, it is. *Gott* will help you.
He'll help Jack. He'll help all of us." She crooned the words into
Sally's ear.

She glanced over at Jack and saw his lips tremble and tears roll
down his cheeks. She stretched out her arm and pulled him into

their embrace. He didn't return the hug, but he didn't resist either.

They stayed like that, huddled together, for the longest time—as if they were the only three people in the world right then. Finally, their tears stopped and the only sound in the room was soft sniffling.

Sally pulled her head back and rubbed at her eyes. Hope let go of them both and squatted on the floor before them.

"Can we go, Hope?" Sally asked. "Can we go to Indiana right away?"

Hope swallowed past the lump in her throat and wiped her damp cheeks. She nodded. "*Jah.* I'll contact *Dat.* I'll explain to him. I'll tell him all you've told me. He'll figure out what to do."

She looked at Jack's swollen eyes. "Are you okay with this, Jack?"

He gave a slow, barely perceptible nod.

Hope stood. "All right, then. We'll get it worked out."

"And Hope, you can see Abram." Sally gave a sharp intake of breath and then smiled. "That will be good, right?"

A warm glow flowed through Hope, and she bent over to squeeze her cousin's hand. "*Jah,* Sally. That will be good."

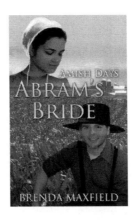

Abram's Bride

One

But without faith [it is] impossible to please [him]: for he that cometh to God must believe that he is, and [that] he is a rewarder of them that diligently seek him.
Hebrews 11:6 (King James Version)

Hope pressed her face against the van window, and her honey-brown eyes took in the harvest-ready fields racing by like falling stars. Her heart fluttered with pleasure at being back in Indiana. She'd been gone just over a month, but it had dragged by like maple syrup.

Beside her, sixteen-year-old Sally and fourteen-year-old Jack sat like sticks, their faces betraying none of what had to be a jumbled mess of emotions. Hope turned to them.

"Are you doing all right?" she asked softly. Over the past weeks, her affection had grown for these two cousins—cousins she hadn't even known existed only a short while before.

Sally sucked in a jagged breath and attempted a smile. Hope put her hand over Sally's clenched fist and gave a gentle squeeze. "It's going to be all right. Everything will be fine."

She leaned around Sally to look at Jack. Moisture hovered in his eyes, and the set of his lips was grim.

"Jack?" Hope's voice was quiet.

His eyes moved, and he stared at her.

"You'll like my little sister, Ann. Did I tell you she has a puppy? Do you like dogs?"

He shrugged. Hope started to take her hand from Sally's, but Sally grabbed it back and held on.

"I always wanted to know more about the Amish." Sally's voice shook. "But never planned to learn like this. You know, without Mom."

Hope's face clouded with sympathy. Had Sally and Jack's mom lived, they wouldn't be moving to her Amish community. Hope still struggled to believe she'd had an unknown aunt—an aunt her own mother had kept a tight-knuckled secret.

Hope pondered Sally's words. Somehow she doubted Sally's mother would have shared anything Amish with her.

The subject of the unknown aunt's split from the family was confusing at best. But now wasn't the time to think further on it, for the Mennonite driver had pulled onto their road. Hope's mind shifted to Abram, her fiancé—the one her family knew nothing about. Her heart fluttered at the thought of his tall good looks, his broad shoulders, and the way his lips pressed into a stubborn line when he wouldn't change his mind about something.

Then her brow creased, and his cherished image gave way to the now constant worry squirming through her belly. While she was gone, Abram had been hurt, his leg broken. A serious break, too; the doctor wasn't sure it would completely heal. In Abram's last letter, he'd said he would need physical therapy, and even that didn't guarantee a full recovery.

Hope exhaled slowly, pressed her face against the window, and whispered a prayer into the glass. Abram *had* to be all right. Wedding season was nearly upon them, and they planned to be published and married by mid-November.

Abram had planned to get his newly purchased farm ready while she was in Ohio. He was to have fixed up the house and gotten furniture—all the while helping his *dat* prepare and bring in the harvest. Now with his broken leg, she wondered how any of it could possibly come together.

Hope couldn't bear the thought of postponing their wedding. She'd waited so long for Abram to share his intentions and reveal his plan to her. She remembered only too well the agonizing days of wondering if he was going to leave their community and live with the *Englisch.*

How those uncertain days had tried her faith. She'd called on God time and time again to help her. Hebrews 11:1 ran through her mind. *Now faith is the substance of things hoped for, the evidence of things not seen.* God had helped her not only believe Him but believe all things would turn out for the good as the scripture promised.

She hugged the knowledge of her engagement to herself. Following Amish tradition, she and Abram hadn't shared their plans with anyone. She hadn't intended for her new cousin Sally to guess that she shared much more than a friendship with Abram. In Ohio, after Hope had heard about Abram's accident, she'd done a poor job of hiding her worry, and it hadn't taken much for Sally to put it together.

"Here we are," the driver said, nodding his balding head. "I'll help with your luggage."

Hope's gaze latched onto the friendly two-story house where she had spent nearly every day of her nineteen years, and her heart warmed at the sight of it. The expansive porch with its white rocking chairs and cozy benches offered her a kind and familiar welcome. She gazed at the roses lining the walk and noted they were freshly trimmed—*mamm's* work for sure.

"We're home," she said with heartfelt cheer. She turned at her cousins. "*Your* new home, too."

The screen door banged open, and her family poured out like bustling chicks.

"You're here!" Hope's little sister Ann ran to meet them with puppy Apple bouncing at her heels.

Mamm stood a bit back, which was odd for her. She wore a look of reticence, and her eyes were weary. Aunt Ruth, also, seemed strangely awkward. But then Hope saw her straighten her spine and march toward Sally and Jack.

"Welcome, children. I'm your Aunt Ruth. We're so glad you're here." Her smile appeared genuine, and she quickly shepherded them up to the porch.

Dat stayed back to finish business with the driver. Mary grabbed Hope's arm and pulled her aside.

"I'm so glad you're home. What are they like?"

"*Shhh.* They're not deaf. But they're fine—nice. You'll see for yourself soon enough."

Ann jabbered on and on about Apple, holding the squirming bundle up to Jack, who gave a barely-perceptible nod in greeting.

"You'll love Apple!" Ann exclaimed. "And we have horses and two cows and three barn cats and lots of chickens."

Ann paused to laugh. "Plus we have raccoons and coyotes and buzzards and mice and snakes—"

Dat joined the family and held up his hand. "Enough, Ann. Let them catch their breath."

Ann leaned close to Jack, as if conspiring. "But those last animals aren't on purpose!"

Jack's lips actually parted in a half-smile then, and Hope's spirits rose. Maybe it was going to be all right after all. She sent up a quick prayer of thanks.

They clambered into the dining room as *Mamm* went to fetch the last of the steaming serving bowls. "We'll eat first and then give you young people a bit of a tour, let you get your bearings."

Two more spots had been added to the table. The long wooden surface had supported many a meal with crowds far bigger than this. But from then on, eight would be the normal number of place settings.

Dat bowed his head. "Let's have a prayer."

Everyone bowed their heads in complete silence. Hope wondered what Sally and Jack were thinking of the silent blessing. In Ohio, she had prayed alone when she was with them. Now she wondered whether she had done a disservice to both God and her new cousins by not urging them to join her.

Dat concluded the silence by exhaling, and they all said amen. Ruth started the bowl of green beans to her left. Sally's eyes darted around the table as if swallowing every last detail. Jack kept his gaze down, only looking up when passed a dish.

Sally put down her fork. "Thank you for taking us in."

Everyone grew still. Hope touched Sally's arm and smiled.

Ann giggled. "Well, of course we did. You're our cousins, aren't you?"

The soft laughter and general agreement that followed seemed to put everyone at ease. Even Mary, who could be sour as a green apple, joined in.

Hope ate quickly, hoping she could figure out a way to see Abram soon. After supper, she jumped up to help Mary clear the dishes. When they were out of earshot, she forced her voice to be casual and asked, "Have you seen Abram? How is he doing?"

Mary peered over Hope's shoulder toward the dining room then focused on her sister. "I've only seen his little sister lately. Mercy said he's cranky as a one-legged rooster. Sets himself on the porch every day with his big old cast and yearns to be out in the fields with his *dat*."

"I need to go over there," Hope said.

"It's going to look mighty odd if you visit Abram alone." Mary studied her sister's face. "So it's true? You're serious about him?"

Hope cheeks grew warm, and their redness would give her away for sure. She turned to plunge her hands into the sink. "Hand me those plates, will you?"

"I knew it! You *are* sweet on him. Do *Dat* and *Mamm* know?" Mary's eyes shone.

"Abram and I have conversed. I don't think it'd be odd for me to go visit a friend who is hurt. Might even take some brownies."

"Take your sugar cream pie. That will get him courting you for sure!"

"Mary, you're awful," Hope teasingly scolded, secretly pleased at the compliment.

"About as awful as you for liking a boy and not telling your sister."

The two of them laughed, and Hope realized just how much she'd missed Mary over the past weeks.

****

Hope didn't have a free moment until it was so late in the evening, she couldn't consider stopping by the Lambrights. After the dishes were finished, she, Mary, and Ann had shown Sally and Jack around the farm. Then Ann insisted they play a quick game of four-square before going in for the night.

After evening prayers, Ruth served them hot chocolate on the porch and *Dat* joined them, telling stories of his childhood. *Mamm* stayed inside, keeping herself busy with some mending. She claimed there wasn't enough light out on the porch to do a proper job.

Hope suspected *Mamm* simply didn't feel comfortable joining them. Again, she wondered what had happened between her *mamm* and Priscilla, and what had made Priscilla flee the community and never return. Priscilla had been *Mamm's* sister, and it couldn't have been easy on *Mamm* to discover there was a niece and nephew she knew nothing about.

Truth be told, the discovery hadn't been easy on anyone.

Jack sat on the porch bench next to Ann. No one but Hope seemed to notice how quiet he was. But then, Ann chattered enough for all of them. Hope sipped her hot chocolate and gazed across the lane to fields that stretched farther than her eye could see in the growing dusk. Crickets chirped and their echoing calls blended with the buzz of cicadas from a nearby oak tree.

Did Abram even know she was back? She and her cousins had left Ohio sooner than planned, and she hadn't had a chance to get a letter off to him. Of course, she might have arrived home before the letter anyway. Hope closed her eyes and imagined Abram sitting on the porch every day full of frustration at not being able to work. Her heart hurt with the thought. Abram was made for work in the fields, and he felt most at home there — with the animals, the land, and the crops.

A warm glow spread through her, and a smile played on her lips. *Dat* reached over and patted her arm with his calloused hand. "Mighty glad to have you home, daughter."

Hope opened her eyes and smiled, surprised at his unusually loving words. "Thank you, *Dat*," she whispered.

With a small, embarrassed cough, he looked away.

Just like her own *dat*, Abram would be a wonderful father to their *bopplis*. She wasn't one to hurry things, but she loved children, and would happily welcome a *boppli* however soon God saw fit to bless them.

Both Sally and Jack were fading, their eyelids drooping. Ruth's rocking chair creaked as she stood. "Time we got you children off to bed. Hope, make sure everyone's well settled."

"*Jah.* Come on upstairs," Hope said. She rose and led everyone into the house.

Perhaps she could arrange to see Abram in the morning. Maybe *Mamm* would like to visit the Lambrights with her. Hope decided to make a sugar cream pie as Mary had suggested. Nothing should seem out of the ordinary if old friends spent a bit of time catching up. And if Abram was on the front porch, well, Hope could dally there without suspicion.

****

As soon as *Mamm* came in from picking a bushel of tomatoes, Hope broached her idea. *Mamm's* eyebrows raised, and her eyes turned sharp and assessing. She set the tomatoes on the kitchen counter. "You've hardly been back five minutes, girl, and already you want to go calling?"

Hope's cheeks grew warm. "I heard Abram Lambright had an accident, and I thought it'd be neighborly to check in on him. And to see Mercy and the others, of course." She rushed to add.

"Mercy and the others, huh?" *Mamm* wiped her hands down her apron and tilted her head. "Is that a sugar cream pie you're making?"

Hope nodded. "It'll be done in an hour. Can we go then?"

"Abram Lambright is a fine young man," Mamm said, taking a tomato from the top of the basket and shining it on her apron. "Your *dat* and I were talking about him just the other day. A hard worker, too. Will make a right fine husband for some sweet girl."

Hope turned to the sink and began scouring her baking utensils.

Mamm gave a small chuckle. "All right, our Hope. We'll go. Would you like to bring your new cousins?"

Hope's hands paused in the suds. She'd wanted to go alone with *Mamm* so she could talk to Abram in private, but how would that appear?

"Of course, *Mamm*." Hope gave the plastic measuring cup a vigorous scrub. "And *Mamm*, we have to arrange school for Sally and Jack. Soon."

"I reckon we do. Don't see the point, though. Eighth grade is schooling enough. Always has been."

"*Mamm,* they're *Englisch.*"

"By blood, they're Amish," *Mamm* stated and walked from the kitchen.

Two

Sitting next to *Mamm* in the buggy, Hope's stomach fluttered as
if filled with fireflies. She clamped her lips together to keep from
giggling with excitement and held the warm pie on her lap with
potholders, not having wanted to wait for it to cool before heading
out. *Mamm* was none too happy with the rush.

"No one visits this early in the morning, Hope. People have
chores to see to."

"That's so, *Mamm*, but this way we get our visit finished and
then can get on with our work the rest of the day."

"Get the visit finished, huh? *Ach*, you're not fooling anyone,
you know." *Mamm* clucked at their road horse, Chocolate. "Nice of
Mary to show Sally and Jack how to tend the chickens. Shame,
though, they couldn't come with us."

The sun was already high and hot. Hope wiped a bead of sweat
from her forehead and decided it might be best to keep quiet the
last few minutes of the ride so as not to give anymore of her
eagerness away.

Chocolate trotted down the Lambright's drive, and there he
was, just like Mary had reported. His left leg, covered with a bulky
white cast, was propped on a low wicker table. When *Mamm* reined
Chocolate to a dusty stop, Abram leaned forward in the rocker,
grinned, and straightened his shoulders. His dark hair fell gently
over his left brow, and he raised his hand in greeting.

He pulled his leg off the table and grabbed his crutches to
stand. "Can I take care of Chocolate for you?" he called, his voice
deep and cool.

"Abram, you sit right on back down," *Mamm* scolded. "I think
after all these years I can see to my own horse."

Hope slid carefully out of the buggy, balancing the pie, her heart beating faster. She glanced at *Mamm*, who had tossed the reins over the hitching post.

"Won't be staying long," *Mamm* announced, whether for Abram's benefit or Hope's, it wasn't clear.

Martha Lambright came to the front door, wiping her hands on a dishtowel. She was all smiles as she greeted them. "Well, Elizabeth Lehman and Hope. How nice of you to come by." The screen door gave a loud squawk as she opened it and beckoned them inside.

Hope handed her the warm pie. "Think I'll stay outside and chat a minute with Abram," she said.

Martha took the pie with one hand and waved a chubby arm toward her son. "You do that. He's bored out of his mind. Could do with some company." She looked down at the pie. "Why Hope Lehman, I declare. Everyone knows your sugar cream is the best in the district. Thank you, child."

Hope reddened at her words, and Martha and *Mamm* disappeared into the house, already chatting about the upcoming harvest.

"Hope," Abram said, his voice thick with emotion. "It's fine to see you."

Hope pulled the porch bench closer to his rocker and sat. "*Ach*, Abram. I'm so sorry. Does your leg hurt?"

His eyes were intent on hers, and the affection there made her breath catch.

"*Nee.* Not much anymore." He shrugged.

"How did it happen?"

Abram raised his head and studied the porch ceiling. When he looked at her again, his eyes were moist.

"It was Sprint. I was hitching her to the buggy like I've done a million times, and she gave out. Just gave out. Collapsed. I didn't move in time. When Doc Milligan came, he said she had an aortic aneurysm."

"She fell on you?" Hope covered her mouth.

"Against my leg. Poor girl. It wasn't her fault."

"And she died when she fell? We all knew she was old, but it's so strange. And too quick."

"Way too quick," Abram said. He shook his head and rubbed the arms of the rocking chair. "Poor Sprint. We couldn't do a thing for her. Doc said her aorta was weak, and it ruptured. We didn't even know there was something wrong until it was too late. Doc said that's the way with an aneurysm."

Abram took a long breath, and Hope knew he still mourned his old mare.

"And your leg?" Hope tensed, fearful of his answer.

"Sprint broke my tibia. She hit me on the way down. Praise *Gott*, I didn't catch her full weight. The doctor decided against surgery and casted it up." Abram paused and took a deep breath. "But he told me I could lose knee motion and stability. And there might be arthritis—long-term arthritis."

He forced a smile, and Hope could see the effort it cost. He continued. "Whoever heard of someone my age with old folks' arthritis?"

He knocked on his cast, as if trying to make light of it.

Hope scooted back, and her eyes searched his. "But it's not for sure, Abram. The doctor just said maybe, right?"

"I'll need physical therapy."

Hope blinked, absorbing the news, and it was a moment before she spoke. "All right, then. In due time, you'll get the cast off and have therapy, and you will be good as new." She leaned forward and grabbed his hand. "Good as new. Do you hear me, Abram Lambright?"

He dipped his head and a heaviness fell over him. "I'm sorry,

Hope. I haven't been to the farm, *our* farm, hardly at all. I wanted to have so much more done."

"But I'm here now, and I can help."

"How would we explain that? You helping me with the house."

"Surely everyone's guessed that you'll be married. Why else would you have bought the place?"

"Perhaps," he said. "But you know it's not our way to make it known till we're published."

"*Mamm* suspects something."

"Did you tell her?"

"*Nee.* But she has eyes."

Abram reached out and took her hand in a warm squeeze. "I feel rotten being laid up like this."

"Abram, we can figure it out. I don't care what shape the house is in. I just want to marry you and make a home."

Abram shook his head. "Do you have any idea of the expense? How this is going to set me back?"

The muscles around his mouth tightened, and his eyes grew shadowed. "I won't have the money to fix up the house."

Hope pressed her hand to her lips and gazed across the yard to the tasseled corn. If she was going to be Abram's wife, she couldn't be a child who fussed when things didn't go her way. And she *had* to be Abram's wife. Her love for him filled her with such intensity that sometimes it was like a sharp pain, welling up through her.

She sat a bit straighter, and her resolve hardened. "We'll figure it out. I can work." Her mind searched for a job idea. Many Amish found positions with the *Englisch* in town. More than a few of her friends served in restaurants, and some of the men worked in factories. She would find something, too. Anything to make this work. Abram caught her hand and pulled it to his lips.

"Hope," he murmured. "I love you so. But, *nee. Nee.*"

She sat back, rebuffed. "What do you mean?"

"We can't start a marriage like that. With me out of commission, and you working to try and support us."

"That's not what I meant!" Hope's words rushed forth. "I will help. That's all, just help. Of course, you won't be out of commission. Don't say such things!"

"Don't you understand? At this rate, I won't be able to make payments." He sat back and his breath seeped from his lips.

She shook her head, and her determination grew. "We can work it out. I know we can."

He showed no signs of relenting. "I won't do it. For two years, I've watched my folks struggle. I've watched *Dat* work himself sick trying to dig out of his financial hole. I've watched *Mamm* put on a happy face and then cry when she thought no one was around. No way I'm putting you through that. *Nee*, Hope. We'll have to wait a year to marry, pray my leg heals and I don't lose the farm."

Hope stared at the stubborn man before her, noted the dogged set of his jaw and the firm look in his eyes. She got it, she did. She understood every word of his reasoning, and she knew the Lambrights had suffered greatly.

But that didn't mean it would happen to them.

She tightened her lips. She'd been taught since birth that in a family, she must obey the man's decisions. And Abram was her fiancé, even though their families didn't know it. She needed to honor his decisions, just as she honored her *dat's* and would honor a brother's if she'd had one. She bowed her head and prayed silently, asking for God's help. She surely needed it, for everything within her cried against being obedient.

"Hope," Abram's voice was tender now. She looked up at his softened expression. "I'm sorry. But we have to do this right."

"We could marry and stay with my parents," she whispered. "Lots of young couples do it."

"Your *dat* has just taken on two new mouths to feed. He doesn't need one more—especially one that's laid up."

Tears welled in Hope's eyes, and she couldn't blink fast enough to make them disappear. "All right, Abram."

She stood and ran her hands down her apron. "But may I look for work? See what's available? I can do that much, can't I?"

Abram tipped his chin and stared up at her with a mixture of exasperation and admiration. Hope held her breath, wondering which emotion would win out. Finally, he shook his head. "If you could only see your face, Hope. It's priceless."

He chuckled. "Seeing you today was like a breath of spring after a blast of winter. You give me hope again."

She snatched up the edge of her skirts and stepped to the screen door. "Well, Hope *is* my name," she said, and her voice was so uncharacteristically saucy that she blushed all the way into the kitchen to find her *mamm*.

****

There was still an hour of light after the evening chores. Hope ran out to the barn and pulled her *mamm's* old bicycle from behind two spare buggy wheels. Now, if she could only get away with no one noticing.

She raised her skirt a couple inches and slid onto the narrow padded bicycle seat.

"Where are you off to?" Sally asked from the barn door.

Hope balanced on one leg. "Just going for a ride."

"I wanted to meet Abram today, but Ruth seemed determined that Mary teach me about chickens. After that, I had to learn about weeding the garden." She studied the palms of her hands. "I'm going to have major blisters."

She looked at Hope. "When are you going back to see Abram? And can I come?"

Hope smiled at her interest. "Of course, you can come."

Sally stepped inside the barn. She was thin, too thin, and the dark circles under her eyes only pronounced her grief-stricken state. She looked ill, and worry for her surged through Hope.

"Can I go with you now? Is there another bike?"

Hope nodded her head toward a second bike hiding behind the wheels. "But I think one of the tires is low," she warned.

Sally rolled out a well-used bike, and sure enough, the back tire was nearly flat. Hope climbed off her bike to reach a tire pump on a shelf. "Do you know how to use this?"

Sally stared at her as if she were daft. "Uh, yeah. I've been riding bikes since age three." Her eyes narrowed, and she gazed off through the barn door. "I'd have my driver's license by now, too, if Mom hadn't…"

She stopped, coughed awkwardly, and knelt down to fasten the pump onto the tire. "Give me two minutes. Where are we going?"

"You won't tell?"

Sally gaped at Hope. "We're sneaking somewhere? You're actually doing something bad?"

Her tone of excitement gave Hope pause.

"*Nee, nee*, of course not," Hope said. "I just don't want it announced." She was annoyed with herself for taking Sally into her confidence, but the girl looked so pathetic, she couldn't help it. Besides, Hope was doing nothing wrong. She simply wanted to peek inside the old Miller farmhouse.

"Okay. It's good," Sally said, dropping the tire pump to the side. "Let's go."

Both girls wobbled slightly over the gravel patch outside the barn. Then they got up some speed and raced out of the drive and onto the road.

"You never said where we're going!" Sally peddled furiously and sped ahead of Hope.

"Wait for me!" Hope called. She'd never gone this fast on a bicycle, and she loved it. She caught up with Sally.

Sally's dark hair flew out behind her. She took her feet off the pedals and stretched her legs straight out in front of her. She laughed and coasted and glanced at Hope with what looked like relief.

"This is fun. And much cooler with the wind in my face!"

Hope wondered if it was unseemly to be riding at such speed. If someone were to see her, she'd be calling bushels of attention her way. Her legs slowed, and she dropped behind.

Sally turned to look and then decreased her speed to match Hope's. "Too fast for you?" she asked, smiling.

"*Jah*," Hope said. "We're almost there anyway."

Ahead of them stretched the old Miller place. The land hadn't been worked for years and it was full of dry weeds as high as Hope. The barn stood tall and sturdy north of the house. There was a smattering of sheds dotting the property to the side and back of the barn, but it was the house that caught Hope's eye.

My home, she thought. *Mine and Abram's.*

The girls came to a stop in a cloud of dust before the porch. A few boards had come loose and were slightly curled at one end. They had been white once, but now the paint was blotchy with large patches completely devoid of any color.

"This place is a wreck," Sally observed. "Why are we here?"

But Hope didn't hear her; she moved as if in a daze. She slipped off her bike and leaned it against the hitching post. Sally followed suit.

"Hope? Earth to Hope…" Sally waved her palm in front of Hope's face.

Hope gave her an absentminded smile. The porch stairs creaked under her slight weight. She put her hand on the front door knob, gave a gentle turn, and wasn't surprised when the door gave way, as most Amish in their community didn't use locks.

"Wait!" Sally cried, scurrying up to join her. "Are you going in?

That's called breaking and entering where I come from!"

Hope stepped into the old house. The linoleum in the entry way was cracked and yellowed. She half-expected cobwebs to entangle her, but there were none. The house stood empty as a cave and nearly as dark.

Sally sashayed around Hope over to the living room windows and tugged on one of the shades. With a snap and a roar, it flipped and rolled up, scattering dust. She coughed and waved at the flying dirt.

Glowing evening light settled into the room. Hope smiled and pivoted slowly, taking it all in.

"Where are we?" Sally asked in a whisper.

"My new home," Hope said, a smile of pure joy spreading across her face.

Sally's eyes widened. "What? You're moving out of your parents' house?"

Hope stepped to Sally and took her forearm with both hands. "*Nee*, not yet. But this is going to be my home."

"You're getting married," Sally said bluntly. "You're marrying Abram just like I thought. I'm right, aren't I?"

Hope blushed and brushed by Sally to continue her tour.

Sally scrambled to catch up. "Do your mom and dad know? How come no one's talking about it?"

"No one knows." In the kitchen, Hope tenderly ran her hand over the cupboards, feeling the well-worn wood that had served others on so many long-ago days. One of the doors jostled and swayed off its hinge. Hope laughed and righted it again.

Sally stood in the middle of the shadowy room and stared at Hope. "I'm the only one who knows you're getting married?"

Hope paused and smiled in contentment at her cousin, hoping with all her heart that Sally was trustworthy. "You're the only one who's guessed. You'll keep my secret?"

Sally's forehead crinkled, and then she smiled back. "I don't get why it's such a big secret, but sure, I'll keep it."

"Thank you, Sally." Hope peered outside through the smudged window over the sink. "It's nearly dark, so we only have a few minutes. Want to take a quick look upstairs before we go?"

Three

That night, the long white curtains fluttered as a cool breeze blew through the bedroom window. Hope lay still and wide awake listening to Mary's gentle breathing beside her. It had to be well past midnight, but Hope couldn't sleep. Her heart beat too quickly with every thought of her new home. It was dirty and needed work, as Abram had said. But she could tell that he'd already been through it and done some cleaning, because there would have been more evidence of critters.

Work he'd done before his broken leg. Was that how time would be divided now: before his broken leg and after?

She remembered his determined expression when he announced they'd have to wait a year to marry. But now that she'd seen the house, now that her heart already lived there, she was certain they could figure it out. Abram had to believe it was possible.

She closed her eyes and prayed.

****

Directly after morning chores, Hope was in the kitchen, flour flying. She'd had her brainstorm during the wee hours of the morning and felt certain she could help raise money to fix up the old farm house.

Mamm stood in the kitchen doorway, watching. "I see we're having sugar cream pie tonight. How many are you making? It's only two more mouths we have around her, daughter."

"I'm going to sell them to the restaurants in town. People say my sugar cream is the best they've tasted." Hope looked down at the lumps of pie crust, hoping her words hadn't seemed too boastful.

Mamm's eyes narrowed, and she studied Hope. "Why the sudden need for money? Are you lacking something?"

"I'm nearly twenty. I thought it time."

Mamm's expression reflected her curiosity. "You do your share around here. That's plenty help."

"I know, *Mamm*. But please, let me do this." Hope wiped her forehead, leaving a streak of flour across her face.

Mamm offered a half-smile. "I'll speak with your *dat*, but I'm thinking he'll raise no objection as long as you get your chores done." She sighed and shifted topics. "Hope, I thank you for spending so much time with Sally. I'm worried about young Jack, though."

Hope glanced beyond her mother to make sure no one else was around. She'd been hoping for a bit of time alone with *Mamm*, for questions about Priscilla still burned in her heart.

"*Mamm*, what really happened?"

Mamm pursed her lips, and the wrinkles around her mouth deepened. Obviously, she knew what Hope meant. *Mamm* leaned against the doorframe, and her whole body seemed to shrink.

Hope hurried to her side and held her mother's arm. "I know it hurt you, *Mamm*. But what happened? Can't I know about *mei aenti*?"

Indecision flashed across *Mamm's* face. Hope waited, praying her *mamm* would share with her, would trust her.

"It's not necessary to know." *Mamm's* voice was hesitant.

Hope pulled her to the kitchen table and helped her to a chair. Tears filled *Mamm's* eyes. "I know Mary was angry with you about Josiah. You know, when he came for supper a while back," she said.

Hope sank into the chair beside her. "You mean when Josiah gave me the attention Mary wanted?"

"*Jah*. I could see what was happening."

"But I didn't want Josiah, *Mamm*. I didn't ask for his favor."

Mamm nodded slowly. "Sometimes, we get what we don't want, and then we want it."

Hope stared at her mother and knew *Mamm* was no longer talking about either Josiah or Mary.

"You and Priscilla?" she asked softly.

Mamm studied her folded hands on the table. One thumb rubbed vigorously over the other. "Me and Priscilla," she repeated.

"So, it was over *Dat*?"

"Priscilla secretly loved him. She was frantic when our *dat* announced that I was to marry him." *Mamm* blinked and shifted in her chair. "Priscilla went to Ruth and poured out her heart. I don't know what she was thinking. Maybe that Ruth would come between us. Or Ruth would tell Benjamin? But by then, I was smitten. Your *dat* was so ... Ruth decided to keep it to herself. She never told me—never told Benjamin. She told no one. And of course, Priscilla never said a word. And then it was too late."

Hope could see *Mamm* was no longer in their kitchen—she was far away, reliving it all over again. A shadow passed over *Mamm's* face, and a small gasp escaped her lips. "Priscilla couldn't, she just couldn't stay and watch. And I didn't know."

"I'm sorry, *Mamm*." From the absent look in *Mamm's* eyes, Hope wasn't sure she'd even heard her.

"Our *dat* refused to look for her ... for Priscilla." *Mamm's* mouth tightened, and she inhaled sharply. "Refused."

Hope's mind flew to her *grossdaadi*. She'd only known him as an angry old man who ranted on about everything wrong with the world. And he would never have anything to do with the *Englisch*. Wouldn't go to their doctors, or their stores, or their businesses. Ever.

So there was more to his anger than she knew. She'd always thought it was just his unforgiving heart and his natural bad temperament. Remorse for her judgment swept through her.

"I'm sorry, *Mamm*," she repeated. She inhaled slowly. "*Mamm*, someday please, won't you tell Sally and Jack their mother's story? I think it might help Sally."

With a quick movement, *Mamm* stood and placed her empty chair firmly back under the table. "Enough talk. Will you need the buggy, then?"

Mamm was back to all business, and Hope knew she would hear no more. She nodded. "*Jah, Mamm*. Late this morning."

"All right, then. I'll speak to your *dat*."

Mamm turned and left the room.

****

Sally went with Hope into Hollybrook. Hope knew of four restaurants that could be interested in her pies. As Chocolate trotted toward town, Sally talked about the coming school year and what it might be like to go to high school in Hollybrook, but Hope had trouble concentrating on her chatter. All she could think of was her *grossdaadi* and how hurt he had to have been when Priscilla disappeared. And it must have been so hard for Priscilla. Where had she escaped to at first? Who had she known? How had she survived in the *Englisch* world? But Priscilla had survived, for her daughter sat right beside her.

Hope guided Chocolate to Amy's Eats just inside the town limits. "Wait here, Sally." Hope picked up one of the fresh pies and disappeared into the restaurant. Within three minutes, she was back. She climbed into the buggy and handed the pie to Sally without a word.

"Well?" asked Sally. "How'd it go?"

"It didn't," Hope answered, crestfallen.

"I should have guessed. You're limping again," Sally observed.

Hope groaned. Since her childhood accident involving a field horse, her weak ankle always gave away her stress.

"But I was sure the restaurant would jump at the chance to buy the pies," she said.

How wrong she was. They'd had a supplier for years and were quite happy with him. Hope clucked her tongue at Chocolate, and they started toward their next target.

In just under an hour, Hope was no closer to earning money than when she'd started out. Actually further away because she'd used a fair amount of ingredients on the six pies sitting in the buggy. As they rolled over the rutted road, she scolded herself for her pride. The scripture said, "Pride goeth before a fall," and she'd surely proven that today.

They were nearly to the edge of town when Sally tugged on her sleeve. "How about there?" she pointed to a gas station with a small market. "Look how many people are stopping."

The lot was indeed full of various vehicles. People emerged from the store sipping on bucket-sized drinks and unwrapping packaged snacks.

"That's not a real restaurant, Sally." Hope snapped the reins gently on Chocolate's back.

"Stop," Sally said with increased fervor. "You've got six pies in here that need sold. If you won't ask them, I will."

Hope pulled on the reins. "You really think they'll want to sell my pies?"

"Can't hurt to try."

Hope guided the buggy to the side of the parking lot. Pairs of eyes goggled them, surely wondering why they'd be stopping at a gas station. Hope was accustomed to being gawked at, but considering the nerve she needed to go inside, she felt particularly self-conscious.

"Want me to go with you? Or instead of you?" Sally asked.

"*Nee*," Hope answered. "I need to do this, but thank you. I'll be right back."

Five minutes later, Hope rushed back to the buggy, a victorious smile covering her face. "Sally, you're wonderful! They want them. All six!"

She reached behind Sally for the pies. "They said a lot of travelers stop for gas here without going into town, so they think there will be a market for Amish pies."

Sally jumped down and grabbed two of them. Hope balanced the others on her arms, and they headed for the store. A few minutes later, they returned to the buggy, and Hope tucked the money she'd received snugly into her purse.

"They're going to sell them for double what they paid you," Sally said as she climbed back onto her seat.

"I know that. But it's still well worth my time." Hope gathered up the reins. "I'm to check back tomorrow to see if they will become a regular customer. Wait till I tell Abram!"

She clucked her tongue, and they were underway.

"There's probably another gas station on the other side of town, you know," Sally said.

Hope grinned. "Let's see how this one goes. Then we'll check it out."

Chocolate trotted down the road where hundreds of buggy wheels had worn grooves into the asphalt. Rows of corn lined the road, tall and unmoving in the still muggy air. Hope's heart warmed with the thought that soon—the following year in fact—with God's blessing, she and Abram would have their own first crop of corn.

A small frown wrinkled her brow. Abram's leg simply had to heal. Farming was grueling enough when fully mobile. Her mind went back to the old Miller house. She yearned to give it a good scrubbing. The windows were filthy and the bathroom … she shuddered. Closing her eyes, Hope visualized it all tidy and neat, with wonderful aromas coming from the kitchen, and the patter of little *boppli* feet trundling down the stairs.

"What are you grinning about?" Sally asked.

"My future," Hope said and breathed a prayer.

****

By the end of the week, Hope had not only secured a permanent pie supplying position at one gas mart, but three. She baked fifteen pies daily—a big order considering she had to fit it around her regular chores. But her greater purpose kept her eager and willing. She developed a system and could whip out the crusts in just over an hour. The different fillings took longer, but she trimmed time off the task every day.

Mamm and Ruth struggled to squeeze in their kitchen work around Hope's baking schedule.

"How long are you going to do this?" Ruth asked, edging sideways between Hope and the counter.

"Hopefully, for quite some time," Hope answered, beating more than a dozen eggs in a large glass bowl.

Mamm gazed at her with raised eyebrows. Hope knew *Mamm* suspected all of the baking had something to do with Abram, but it wasn't their way to push too hard into personal business. And it wasn't as if Abram was coming around regularly taking Hope for rides in a courting buggy.

These days, Abram saved his energy to tend the animals, hobbling between the barn and the grazing field on his crutches.

"*Mamm*, I need to run an errand after supper. Do you need me for anything?" Hope asked, pouring fresh milk into the beaten eggs.

"I want you to check the coop fence. Your *dat* is too busy in the fields right now, and it looked suspicious when I last gathered eggs. Seems like something's been digging."

"All right, *Mamm*. And after that?"

"I imagine it would be all right."

Four

Mamm was right. Animals had been digging at the west end of the coop. Hope thought it might be raccoons. Something had pulled and flipped the sod into a jumble. Hope shoveled dirt into the hole, stamped down the sod, and set a wooden plank on top of the area. *There, that should do for now,* she said to herself as she carried the shovel back to the shed.

Ann and Jack emerged from the open door, packing hoes over their shoulders.

"We checked on Chocolate earlier," Ann told Hope. "I showed Jack how to brush her down."

Hope studied Jack's face. Some of the dark shadows had cleared, and he looked almost content. Hope wanted to gather Ann in a hug of gratitude. All day, every day, Ann towed Jack and Apple around, and it seemed to be the best thing for all concerned. Hope had never known any person or animal who wasn't won over by Ann's infectious giggle and exuberant happiness.

Hope hurried to the barn to extract *Mamm's* bicycle and rode off toward the Lambrights. She felt a bit guilty for not taking Sally, but she and Abram weren't meeting at his house. They planned to meet at the edge of the Lambright's property, where there was a small stand of oak trees. Hope had been doubtful about Abram going so far on his leg, but he'd assured her it was fine.

As she pedaled nearer the trees, she saw a flash of blue. Her heart quickened and she increased her speed. She rolled over the lumpy dirt into the shade of the trees. Abram was leaning against the trunk of the biggest oak, and an easy smile played at the corners of his mouth.

She jumped off the bike and balanced it against a stump. She turned to him, her eyes alight. "Abram! You made it!"

He set his crutches aside and held out his hands to her. She stepped close and put her hands into his. They gazed into each other's eyes, and every cell in Hope's body tingled with excitement.

"How is your leg today?" she asked.

He leaned forward and brushed his lips against her cheek. His kiss sent the pit of her stomach into a wild swirl. His face was so close that his breath fluttered over her mouth, and she breathed him in. His lips whispered against her cheek once more, and then he moved ever so slightly to her mouth. Her heart beat hard and without thought, her lips moved under his. She heard a low sound in the back of his throat, and he pulled her roughly into his embrace. She snuggled her head against his broad chest, and their breath came in soft gasps. He pressed his cheek on the top of her *kapp,* and they continued to stand for a long moment, until he gently pushed her from him.

"*Ach*, Hope." His voice was thick and unsteady. "You are so beautiful."

She lowered her thick lashes, overcome by his words and his admiration. He cupped her chin in his hand and brought her liquid gaze back to his. His eyes caressed her softness, and then he shuddered slightly and straightened his shoulders.

"We can't get carried away or do something unseemly." He inhaled slowly, paused, and then smiled. "You asked about my leg. I go back to the doctor next week. But it's not bothering me as much."

He leaned heavily on his good leg. "Except it's starting to itch. In fact, the itching is driving me mad." His gentle laughter rippled through the air.

Hope grinned. "Abram, I'm sorry. You poor thing. But you truly think it's better?"

"It's better," Abram answered, his voice deep and certain.

"Now what's this about you and pies I keep hearing about?"

Hope bit her lip. He'd already heard? She had wanted to be the one to tell him—she should have known that the Amish gossip line would reach him first.

"I'm earning money now, Abram." She hoped he would understand why she had done it and not be angry with her. She sympathized about his *dat's* struggles, but maybe this would help Abram see a different possibility—even though she knew he wanted to be the sole provider. "I'm selling pies five days a week. I don't know how long they'll keep wanting them. It will probably slow down during the winter months."

"Who is 'them'?"

"Three gas markets in Hollybrook." She clasped his arm. "I like it, Abram. And I'm earning money for us. To help."

A scowl touched his face. "I don't like you thinking you have to work. That's not the way I want it to be, Hope. We need to wait."

Hope grew quiet. She looked at the set of his jaw and the intensity of his gaze. She loved him for his strength, even for his stubbornness. She wanted to honor him, but she knew that she could help. She *was* helping. Wasn't there a way to do both?

She licked her lips and tried to find the right words. Abram's gaze hadn't left her face, but she saw the faintest hint of a smile begin to tip the edges of his mouth. She waited, and he shook his head with a look of begrudging amusement.

"What am I to do with you, Hope? Your face is such an open book. Every emotion you feel is stamped on it for all the world to see. You're angry with me now, *jah*?"

She smiled and relief at his improving mood spread through her. "Maybe. A little. I want to help. I want to marry this year."

He gathered her into his arms, and she once more felt his strong, quick heartbeat. He eased back from her and stroked her cheek with his calloused hand. "Hope," he said, and his voice caught. "Hope."

Hope took in every detail of his precious face. The touch of his lips on hers again sent shivers down her body. His kiss was as tender and light as a summer breeze. When he released her, he pressed the palm of her hand to his mouth as if drinking in her sweetness.

"Is there a chance, Abram? A chance we can still marry this fall? During the wedding season?"

Abram moved her hand to his heart where he clasped it hard. "With *Gott*, there is always a chance. But, please, don't set your heart on it."

Hope fell against him again, and they held each other for a long moment until Abram kissed the tip of her nose.

"We can't stay here forever, Hope. It'll be dark soon, and it won't be safe for you to ride."

"I know." She paused, took a deep breath, and added, "I went to the house. Will you let me work on it?"

Abram's eyebrows raised. "So, you saw it? Why am I not surprised? And what do you mean work on it?"

"Mostly scrub it from top to bottom. It's not that bad, Abram. Truly, it isn't."

"There's a leak in the roof over the back bedroom. I put a tarp up weeks ago, but it's only temporary. And there are problems with the foundation. I need to get jacks under it. And that causes problems in the cellar."

"Is it unsafe?"

He rubbed his chin. "No. Not for a while yet. But the foundation must be fixed. And I can't do it. Well, at least, not yet."

Hope clasped his hand. "We can ask for help."

Abram shook his head. "It's harvest season. No one has time for anything but the crops."

Hope sighed. "I suppose you're right."

"There is one thing we can do. We can pray. *Gott* has everything in control. He's proven it so many times." A thoughtful smile curved his mouth. "Let's pray together, and ask for His help, and then you must go."

****

The following Tuesday afternoon after delivering her pies, Hope stopped at Feed & Supply. She put a bucket, mop, broom, scrub brush, rubber gloves, and cleanser onto the expansive counter. Mrs. Troyer glanced at it all and then at Hope.

"Spring cleaning in the fall, dear?" Her high-pitched voice warbled. She raised her eyebrows so high, Hope half-expected them to fly off her face.

"Cleanliness is next to Godliness," Hope quipped.

Mrs. Troyer chuckled and rang her purchases up on the battery-generated register. "*Jah*, 'tis true, 'tis true."

Hope gathered her things and returned to the buggy. She gently slapped the reins and Chocolate clip-clopped toward the old Miller place. When she drew the buggy near the porch, she craned her neck, hoping no one was in the vicinity to notice. How would she possibly explain why she was taking supplies to Abram Lambright's newly-purchased farm? She scrambled out of the buggy and took all the cleaning supplies inside. She dropped them in the corner of the living room, barely taking the time to glance around. Even so, her heart quickened with excitement simply from walking over the threshold. Without stopping to revel in the pleasure, she hurried back to the buggy and headed for home.

She'd come back later to start the cleaning.

Sally was standing next to the hen house when Hope pulled into the drive. She waved at Hope and went to meet her at the barn.

"Did you sell all your pies?" she asked. "Next time, take me, okay?"

Hope jumped down and unhitched Chocolate. "All right."

Sally pressed her lips together and turned away. Hope saw her tremble and touched her shoulder. "What's wrong?"

Sally slowly faced Hope, her expression contorted and tears flowing. "You're asking me what's wrong?" Her voice shook. "What's *not* wrong? I'm stuck on this stupid, *stupid* farm all day long, that's what's wrong!"

Hope gaped as if slapped. She'd thought Jack was the one having problems adjusting. She hadn't realized Sally was suffering so deeply.

Sally's chest heaved, and her body stiffened. "I can't stand it here! There's nothing to do! No friends! I'm even looking forward to school in pathetic Hollybrook. That's how desperate I am!"

Sally's face burned red and her breath came in gasps. "I'm sorry, Hope" she muttered. "I'm sorry."

She turned and half-ran toward the cluster of oak trees behind the house. Hope slapped Chocolate on the bottom, sending her into the barn and her stall. She quickly latched the gate and hurried after Sally.

Sally had collapsed on the dirt beneath a towering oak. Her head was bowed and muffled sobs flowed, punctuating the air with her pain. Hope dropped beside her on the ground. "Sally," she crooned, "I'm so sorry. I thought you were adjusting, even liking it here."

Sally hiccupped but didn't raise her head.

"What can I do? How can I help you?"

Sally shook her head over and over. "You can't," came her muffled reply.

Hope rested her hand on Sally's knee and simply sat with her. She waited while Sally's sobs slowly turned into sniffles.

Hope tucked her legs beneath her and breathed in the humid air and wished for a breeze. Her neck was sticky and moisture gathered on her upper lip. She sent up a quick prayer for wisdom.

"Sally?" Her voice was a whisper. "You're the only one who knows."

Sally tipped her head an inch and looked at Hope through scraggly brown strands of hair.

"You're the only one who knows about Abram and me. Not even Mary."

Sally leaned her forehead against Hope's shoulder, and Hope rubbed her back lightly. "Do you want to clean my new house with me? It has to be a secret."

"I'm not a baby—I know what you're trying to do." Sally swallowed hard. "You're trying to make me feel better because I'm your secret keeper."

"You're more than my secret keeper, Sally. You're my cousin, my dear cousin. I've grown awfully fond of you."

"Still trying," Sally said.

Hope grinned. "It's working, *jah*?"

Sally bit her lip, and then offered Hope a feeble smile. "A little."

"So? Will you help clean?"

Sally nodded, and they both got up and brushed the leaves and dirt off their backsides.

"We'll leave after we tidy up the supper dishes," Hope said. "On bikes."

Five

Hope's hands cramped from gripping the scrub brush so hard. Kneeling, she put all her weight into the last corner of the kitchen floor and then sank back on her haunches.

"Done!" she exclaimed.

Sally peered at her from behind a cupboard door. "It looks good, Hope. 'Course now we have to walk back across it."

"I'll scrub the bottom of our feet then!" Hope laughed.

Sally was proving to be a hard worker, and Hope felt deep gratitude. They'd done an amazing amount of work in a couple hours.

"*Mamm* and Ruth will be looking for us. We'd better get back." Hope stood and tried to stretch the kinks out of her legs and back.

The front door banged shut and Sally and Hope stared at each other in shock. Hope hurried from the kitchen and came to an abrupt halt when she saw who it was.

"What are you doing?" cried Mary, her face full of accusation.

Hope's mouth dropped open. "How did you know we were here?"

"*And Sally is with you?*" Mary's icy stare took in Sally.

"Does *Mamm* know we're here?" Hope asked.

Mary's shoulders rose and tension filled the room. "How could you?" she said, her voice tearful. "You brought Sally but not your *own sister?*"

Hope's breath seeped out. She had been sneaking about — which was bad enough. But the fact that she hadn't taken her sister into her confidence was plain wrong. And hurtful.

She took an awkward step toward Mary. "I'm so sorry. You're right."

Sally cleared her throat. "If it helps, Hope didn't tell me. I guessed."

Mary leveled a bitter look her way.

Hope mouthed a *thank you* to Sally and then turned to her sister. "Sally's telling the truth. I didn't really tell her." She dropped her gaze. "But you're still right. I should have told you."

Hope took Mary's hands, but Mary shook them loose and began walking around the room, gazing at everything. "So this is Abram's new place."

Hope nodded.

"And going to be yours, too, I assume."

Even feeling guilty about Mary's pain, Hope couldn't completely stop the joy flowing through her at the words.

"*Jah*," she whispered.

Mary stopped her inspection and stared at her sister. She was quiet for a long moment, and Hope could see her struggle. Forgiving others had never come easy for Mary, and this time was evidently no exception. Hope held her breath and waited to see which way the wind would blow.

After a large gaping silence, Mary finally said, "We could have a cleaning frolic."

Hope's brows rose in amazement.

"A frolic?" Sally asked. "What's that?"

Mary ignored Sally and kept her gaze steady on Hope.

Hope turned to her cousin. "It's basically a work party. We all get together and laugh and joke and work. It's our way. We help each other."

Hope looked back to Mary, her excitement rising. "Are you serious, Mary? Even after the way I behaved?"

Mary walked to a wall and ran her hand down it. "We could get this place shining in no time. New paint, too."

Hope stared at her and the sound of the crickets outside grew more insistent. And then with a rush of emotion, she said, "Mary, you're the best sister ever. I don't deserve it, but thank you."

"What else needs done?" Mary asked.

"The foundation needs work and so does the roof."

"We need men for that and with harvest time here, it won't happen. But, later, it could." Mary's face was solemn. "I'll get the frolic planned. Abram's sister can help. If you take charge, everyone will know why."

Hope shook her head in wonder. "Thank you, Mary. Thank you." Hope marveled at how severely she had underestimated her sister. Had she been that consumed with her own issues?

"How'd you get here?" Sally asked.

"I walked. I figured Hope disappearing had something to do with Abram, and then the thought of his farm came to me. It took me a while to get here."

"You can balance on the back of my bike on the way home," Sally offered. "I'm an expert at riding double. Used to cart Jack around everywhere."

Mary agreed, and the three of them headed home, racing against the dark.

****

Mary and Abram's sister Mercy were able to put the frolic together within a week. Because of the harvest, the timing was bad, but a group of women felt so sorry for Abram Lambright that in true Amish fashion, they gathered together.

Hope stayed in the background of the planning as best she could, but when Saturday morning came, she was there scrubbing and painting and laughing with the rest of them. By early afternoon, Hope was astonished at what had been accomplished. After sweeping up the last of the mess, she leaned on the broom handle and marveled at how much more homey everything felt.

Mamm came to stand next to her. "Mary's a good sister," she stated.

Hope's breath caught. Of course, *Mamm* would have guessed all this was really for her.

Mamm smiled and patted Hope on the shoulder. "As I've said, Abram is a fine young man. This house will serve him well."

Hope glanced at her mother. *Mamm's* face was serious, but there was the hint of a twinkle in her eye. Hope's heart warmed to see *Mamm* acting almost normally again after all the shock of Priscilla's passing.

Hope knew the twinkle was there for her. For her *and* Abram. She gave a deep and gratifying sigh. Surely, she and Abram could be published in October now.

All of the women returned to their own homes and chores. Ruth drove Mamm, Sally, Ann, and Mary in the buggy. Hope stayed back as she had ridden a bike, hoping to have a moment alone in her future home.

She set the broom against the kitchen wall and surveyed the room. It was now a pale blue. The cupboards looked almost new after a fresh coat of white paint. The floor was well-worn, but Hope loved knowing how many people had used the kitchen in the past. *Her* kitchen, the heart of her future home. She closed her eyes and visualized herself cooking, and canning, and serving, with little *bopplis* tugging on her skirt, completely underfoot.

She grinned.

"What are you smiling about?" Abram's rich, deep voice teased.

She twirled to face him. "How did you get in here? Why didn't I hear you?"

"I saw your bike so I came in especially quiet." He laughed at the embarrassed look on her face. "Can I hope you were smiling because you love the house?"

"*Nee.*"

At her denial, a look of disappointment shadowed his face.

"I was smiling because I love both the house *and* you."

Abram grabbed her around the waist and pulled her close. She rested her head against his heart. Then she pulled back.

"Wait! You shouldn't be traipsing around on that leg, should you?"

"No way I was going to miss what you ladies and your frolic accomplished." With his hand still on her waist, his gaze traveled the room. "It looks remarkable."

"Good enough to live in, right?" she asked.

He shook his head and laughed, and the sound of his pleasure filled her with delight.

"You won't give up, will you? Is this what I've got to look forward to all the days of my life?" he asked, turning her to him so he could gaze deeply into her eyes. "*Ach,* Hope, I'm so eager to make you my bride."

"My pies bring in steady money now. And look, you're up and about. Things are improving. *Gott* is answering prayer."

"I never doubted *Gott* would answer prayer. But I never wanted to be foolhardy, either. I want to do this right—I don't want to end up suffering like *Dat* and *Mamm.*"

"But we're not your *dat* and *mamm.*" Hope raised her hand and gently touched his cheek. "We're you and me. Things don't have to be the same for us as they were for them. I don't want to be crazy either, but you make me feel safe, Abram Lambright."

"I never want you to feel otherwise." His voice broke with huskiness.

"And I won't," she murmured.

He grabbed up his crutches and the two of them wandered from the kitchen. "I'm well pleased with your work. Amazed even. It was all Mary's planning, wasn't it? And Mercy's?"

Hope nodded. "Mostly Mary. She knows, Abram, and I feel

badly I didn't tell her straight away. She would have kept our secret. She's my sister, and we're close. I should have told her."

"I've been to the doctor, Hope."

Hope swirled to him. "What did he say? Is your leg going to be all right?"

He rested his strong hands on her shoulders. "I need physical therapy like I thought. Nearly everyone with this type of break does, so it's not unusual. But our doctor knows a therapist who works with the Amish. One who understands that we don't have health insurance and charges accordingly."

"*Ach*, Abram, that's wonderful!"

"It will help, no doubt." He adjusted the crutches under his arms. "But my knee may never be sound again, and I have to be prepared for that. I don't know if I can handle all that needs to be done on a farm. Not just now, but in the future."

The worry on his face and in his eyes made Hope's throat constrict. This man standing before her filled her with admiration.

"Then we'll have sons." Hope spoke eagerly. "Many, many sturdy, beautiful sons, God willing."

"No guarantee of that, Hope."

"No guarantee of anything, Abram."

She stood tall and resolute and in the depths of her heart, all apprehension, all worry about the future, dissolved into nothing. Maybe she *was* foolish or foolhardy, as Abram called it, but she felt a heavenly confidence that together she and Abram would be able to handle anything life brought their way.

Abram inhaled slowly, and a faint light started in the depths of his black eyes. "Perhaps, Hope. Perhaps, we can do it. *Gott* and you and me."

She nodded. "*Jah*." Her voice was soft and clear.

His grip on her tightened. "I ask you again, Hope. Will you marry me?"

"I answer you again, Abram. *Jah,* I will marry you."

"Will you marry me in two months?"

A cry of relief broke from her lips. "*Jah,* Abram. Two months. *Jah.*"

He took her hand solidly in his. "All right, then. I hope I'm not being unwise. Shall we inform our families?"

"Most of mine already knows," she said and laughed. "But, *jah,* let's inform our families."

Together, they walked outside—he hobbling, and she steady by his side.

Epilogue

The morning had been ripe with a flurry of activity. The three-hour sermon had now finished, and Hope stood with Abram before the Bishop in her newly-made wedding dress. The fabric was the color of the sky on a clear day, and Hope had lovingly sewn every stitch. A surge of gratitude flowed through her as the Bishop asked the two of them questions, and they affirmed their commitment to each other and to God. Hope's eyes grew large and liquid as she gazed at Abram's dear face, and she found it impossible not to return his captivating smile.

She glanced at her family and love for them filled her chest nearly to the point of bursting. Sally grinned at her from her position as one of the attendants, and Hope realized again how much she'd grown to love her new cousin. A movement caught her eye, and she noticed Abram's relative Josiah studying her face. A flash of memory caught at her. She well remembered when he had asked her to ride with him after the Sunday singing. Now she wondered—did Josiah still have feelings for her?

Josiah nodded and with a teasing raise of his brows, she knew all was well. She caught Mary's gaze and saw tears in her sister's eyes. Hope's heart lifted and she decided to play matchmaker right after the wedding—Josiah was a fine catch, and Mary was already smitten with him.

Abram caught her hand, and together they faced their friends and family. Abram leaned slightly on his cane, evidence that his leg was some better and healing. Uncertainty still remained as to whether it would heal completely, but at that moment, at that beautiful love-filled moment, Hope knew to the depths of her being that no matter what happened, no matter what the outcome, everything would work to the good as God promised.

A Note from the Author

If you **love** to read **Amish Romance**, please visit:

http://brendamaxfield.com/newreleasenotice.html

to find out about all **New Hollybrook Amish Romance Releases!**
We will let you know as soon as they become available!

If you enjoyed *Amish Days: Hope's Story* would you
kindly take a couple minutes to leave a positive review on Amazon?
It only takes a moment, and it truly makes a difference. I would be
so grateful! Thank you!

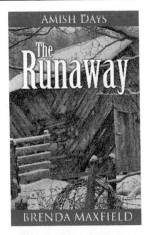
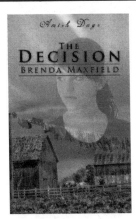

Hope's Story

More Amish romances are always coming your way! You can stay informed:

http://brendamaxfield.com/newreleasenotice.html

**Thank you!
You are appreciated!**

http://www.brendamaxfield.com